Mail Order Rescue

Book Two of
Mail Order Bluebonnet Brides

Charlotte Dearing

Author's note: My stories are clean, wholesome love stories set in late 19th century Texas. The hero is strong, successful, and flawed, in ways he doesn't realize until he meets the heroine. In the end, my heroes and heroines find a path to happiness through perseverance and faith.

Chapter One

Emily

Emily knew there was no escaping what was about to come. She stepped back and lowered her eyes to the floor, staring at anything other than her uncle.

Whenever her uncle berated her in front of a customer, he'd taunt her about her empty head. The words stung, but he made the insults even more painful by making sure everyone in the store heard. Worse yet, he'd list her shortcomings while he kept his beady eyes fixed on her neckline.

"How difficult is it to cut a bolt of cloth, stupid girl?" Uncle Roy shouted.

Emily winced. Her hands often shook when her uncle came near. She'd tried to cut a straight line, but instead left a jagged edge, and now the fabric was ruined.

The customer, a woman who came in once a week for sewing supplies, looked at Roy in wide-eyed alarm. "Now look here," she said, trying to come to Emily's aid.

"I'll manage my affairs as I see fit," Roy snapped.

The woman gaped. Emily felt sorry for her. Roy shouted at customers any time the mood came along. Especially female customers. What did it matter if he upset them? There was no other place for them to shop. Nelson's Mercantile was the only general store for miles. It was Roy's personal kingdom, and everyone, including the customers, were mere underlings.

Outside, the dark, stormy skies lent a dismal gloom to the mercantile. Rain poured off the roof, splashing onto the walkways. A chill hung in the air, and not just from Roy's icy tone.

"I'm sorry, Mrs. Wilson," Emily said quietly. "I'm happy to pay for the material out of my own wages."

"It's no trouble, dear. I intend to pay for the material myself." The woman squared her shoulders and leveled a hard look at Roy.

Roy snarled at Emily. "Get out of my sight."

Emily gave the woman an apologetic look and hurried to the back of the store. She couldn't ever do anything right. Not as far as he was concerned. For two months, she'd lived with her uncle and aunt. It had started well enough, but over time he'd become increasingly antagonistic. If a cowboy smiled at her, she was being a harlot, like her mother. If she kept her eyes down, he accused her of being sullen and running off customers.

She was nineteen but had nothing to her name. When her mother died, she'd begged her aunt to take her in, just for a short while. The arrangement had grown more miserable by the day. Soon, she promised herself, she'd leave Magnolia, get on a train and head west. The tension in her shoulders lessened as she imagined standing on a beach, listening to the breaking waves and watching the sun sink on the western horizon.

What she'd do once she got to California wasn't something she thought much about. From what she'd heard, San Francisco was a boomtown. She was sure she'd find some sort of work. It didn't matter much. Anywhere was better than living with her aunt and uncle.

Darting into her room, she snatched her drawing pad and pencils and headed to the back porch. The rain had let up, but there was still a cold drizzle. She'd keep dry, sitting under the overhang.

The back porch had become a tiny sanctuary for her. She'd discovered it the day after she arrived. It was outside, which was wonderful, but she also knew she'd be alone. Uncle Roy and Aunt Carol never came out. There was no furniture, but she's made a stool out of an overturned crate.

A few days ago, someone had moved her crate and set up a small, round table and several chairs. At first, she'd imagined it might have been Uncle Roy. After all, who else could it be? But then she realized he would be the last person to show her any kindness. Aunt Carol wouldn't have put the table there either. Carol made it clear that she only wished to do her minimal familial duty by taking her in, but nothing more.

The yard behind the mercantile belonged to the livery barn. There was always plenty to see. Men hitched wagons, repaired tack and groomed horses. The horses provided good subject matter for Emily's drawings. The yard was quiet now, just a few horses and a single black mule. Standing in the rain, the animals looked a little bedraggled. She wondered if they were cold and wished someone would take them inside.

She opened her sketch pad and began to draw the chestnut standing by the rail. Beginning with his head, she drew the line of his handsome profile, a roman nose adorned with a wide blaze. His ears and lips were slack, and she realized with amusement that, despite the rain, the horse dozed.

His neck didn't have much of an arch, not while he rested. She'd seen him many times before, though, and knew how handsome he was. She imagined him galloping along a Texas trail with a cowboy on his back. With his pretty markings he had a distinguished air about him. She stopped her pencil to look up and study his features.

"May I see what you're drawing?"

She yelped with fright. A man stood not more than a few paces away. Rain dripped from the brim of his cowboy hat. He wore trousers, a white shirt and a leather vest. He was plainly dressed but she was certain he was no livery stable hand. He carried himself with a commanding presence. A wave of emotion washed over her, a mixture of surprise and anger. She'd been so engrossed in her drawing she hadn't heard him approach.

He regarded her with vague interest, arching his brow at her outburst.

"Well?" he asked again.

The man reminded her of her mother's gentleman callers. Much younger, of course, but he had the same imperious expression. He held out his hand, waiting for her to hand over her drawings.

"You may not," she said archly.

The man blinked. His hand lowered and for a moment, the two looked at each other without speaking. He thinned his lips with clear disapproval. Worry wrapped around her heart. She didn't know who this man was, but he looked like he might be one of Magnolia's more important citizens. His boots were made of some fine leather with expensive stitching. His trousers, while a simple fabric, were spotless. His shirt was pressed, probably by a maid. He wasn't a man who toiled in the dirt or filth. He was somebody, which meant he might cause problems for her if she angered him.

Part of her didn't care. Much.

"You shouldn't sneak up on people," she snapped. She would be wise to use a gentler tone, a more submissive voice, but he'd frightened her. Then he had the bad manners to ask about her drawings. Who did he think he was?

"I said hello. Twice."

"You did?"

He nodded. "I thought you heard."

"What made you think that?"

"Because you made a sound."

Emily narrowed her eyes. "A sound?"

He shoved his hands in his pockets and leaned against the railing, a slow smile curving his lips.

"You said mmph."

The man had to be crazy. Worse, despite the rain, he seemed ready to settle in for a visit. Panic flared, burning her chest. If Roy came out and found her talking with a man, a stranger at that, there was no telling what he'd do. And the man before her might have frightened her and even angered her, but she didn't want him to hear Roy hurl insults at her.

She gathered her things. "I'm sure you're mistaken. I didn't hear you, so it's not possible that I replied."

He nodded. "All right."

A spark of anger flickered inside her. The man was so cocksure, so arrogant and so very certain that he could simply intrude in her life. She knew all too well the type of man who regarded women as mere trinkets. All of them began conversations with a kind smile, an almost-polite word, hiding what they really wanted. Her mother lived her life finely attuned to this type of man. Emily could hardly keep from grimacing at the memory.

At least men like Uncle Roy didn't hide their contempt for the weaker sex.

5

"Emily," her aunt's sharp voice came from behind her. Carol Nelson strode onto the porch, giving her niece a hard look. "What are you doing?"

Before Emily could reply, her aunt caught sight of the man. Her entire demeanor changed from anger to courtesy. She schooled her features, coaxing a smile from her hard mouth. "Mr. Calhoun, I didn't know you were out here. I hope my niece wasn't disturbing you."

Carol delighted in telling Roy what a worthless girl she was, how she not only pilfered money when she did the store's books, but she shirked her duties. Now she'd have a new grievance. Never mind that Roy had sent her out of the store.

"Your niece was not disturbing me." The man's tone was cool. The smile from a moment ago had faded as he regarded Carol with unmistakable disdain.

Carol's face colored. She pursed her lips and narrowed her eyes at Emily. "You shouldn't be out here. I'm certain there is plenty for you to do in the store."

Emily collected her things. There was no use explaining what had happened. Carol would only become angrier. Emily didn't want to be further humiliated in front of the man in the cowboy hat. She returned to the store. She felt Mr. Calhoun's eyes on her as she left the porch. Awareness of his gaze made her shiver. Carol caught up with her as she put her pad and pencil away in her small bedroom.

"You'd be wise to keep away from Baron Calhoun," Carol hissed. "He's exactly the type of man your mother would have dallied with."

Emily kept her gaze averted. "I won't speak to him again."

"I should hope not. He owns the Magnolia Bank, and half the town, including this very building. He could raise our rent anytime he wanted. Poor Roy would have no choice but to pay.

6

Even worse, Roy took out a loan from Mr. Calhoun to start the store."

Emily nodded.

"Men will always flock to you, but none of them for respectable reasons. They'll notice the strange, uncommon color of your eyes. Same as my sister. Men thought her eyes were special because they were violet colored. They weren't anything special."

Emily shook her head. "No, they weren't."

She'd hoped her soft response would deflect some of Carol's wrath. Instead, it seemed to burn hotter.

"Even worse," Carol seethed. "Men will take one look at you and sense the stain of your past."

Emily bit her tongue. She had no stained past. None. But Carol loved to drill the point that the shame of her mother's life would always shadow her every move. Somehow people would look at her and *know*. The logic behind her accusation was never explained. Emily never dared question her aunt on this point, or any other. Probably because, even though it made no sense, part of her believed it with even more conviction than Carol.

"You're right," she murmured. "I'll try to do better."

"You should write to some of those men looking for a mail-order bride," Carol said.

This again.

"You're right," Emily said.

Never...

Emily had no desire to marry. From an early age, she'd seen the worst in men. The lying. The cheating. The violence. She'd promised herself to never bind herself to a man. If she never married, she'd never suffer at the hands of an unfaithful husband. The rain had resumed, drumming down on the roof.

Emily's spirits felt as colorless as the gray, dismal day. She waited for Carol to say something more.

After a moment, she lifted her gaze to find that Carol had left. She breathed a sigh of relief and finished putting her things away. Shadows filled the small room. Tucked under the stairwell, the room's ceiling tilted at odd angles. She edged to the corner where her chest of drawers sat. Inside the drawers were the dresses her mother had bought her in hopes that she might catch the eye of a wealthy "friend". Emily never wore them and wanted nothing more than to burn them and render the shameful memory to ash.

The voluminous gowns served a purpose, though. She hid her small savings in the folds of silk and satin, a tiny purse that held the sum of her dreams. Kneeling beside the bottom drawer, she ran her fingers along the back edge. When she found the small purse, she ran her fingers over the fabric. The purse held eight dollars, half of what she needed for train fare to California.

She didn't know what she'd do when she got there, but had long ago decided, she'd leave that in God's hands. She fervently hoped he'd show her a path. Living with Roy and Carol was a trial, but brighter days awaited, if only she could save enough money for a ticket to freedom.

Chapter Two

Baron

Baron should have been halfway home by now, but instead he remained in Fort Worth one more night, enduring his lawyer's hospitality. It wasn't all bad. He dined on prime rib and other fine foods, but dinner required him to be sociable. He would have preferred to return to Magnolia. But if he'd turned down the invitation, he would have caused hard feelings. He tried his best to avoid giving offense, especially since there was something he wanted from Charles Stanton.

Baron wanted an introduction to the Presidio Cartel, a mining company. Based in Houston, the group controlled most of the silver mines in west Texas. Stanton represented the company and had promised him a letter of introduction. There was a rumor that the group had run into financial trouble, in which case Charles's goodwill would hardly be necessary. The cartel members would be only too eager to receive Baron.

Still, diplomacy never hurt.

Or at least not for long.

Baron had always done well for himself. His first job was shoveling coal for Southern Pacific Rail Line. They'd hired him because of his brawn. He left the railroads and worked as a bounty hunter, only pursuing the criminals with the highest bounties. When he tired of that, he took a job as a runner for a bank.

He worked. He saved. He studied at night.

His sharp eye for opportunities paid off and now he didn't work in banks. He owned them. He was ready for the next step. Mining and shipping would reap rewards far greater than banking and ranching.

The dinner conversation, polite but utterly boring, faded from his thoughts. While Baron should have been listening to his host's wife talk about her family's timber interests in East Texas, he let his mind wander to a subject that interested him more.

The girl from the mercantile.

The girl with the violet eyes.

Emily.

Never had he seen eyes that color. And never had a woman tried to cut him down to size with a single, haughty look. Most women tried to charm him. They offered admiring glances, coy, flirtatious remarks, and subtle suggestions of what could be his, if only he were to ask.

Tonight, for example, the young lady sitting across from him at the dining table was an example of feminine charms and grace and wiles. Katherine Stanton, Charles' daughter was an only child, and stood to inherit a sizeable fortune one day.

Her mother, Susanna Stanton, droned on about the forests and mills on her family's vast property.

Katherine smiled at him and batted her lashes. Her eyes were pretty enough, but nothing he wanted to gaze into for the next thirty or forty years. Still, there was the subject of Katherine's inheritance. Her money would allow him to buy more grazing land. More cattle. More of everything.

After all, money did make the world go around.

He'd figured that out from an early age. His father had been a poor man, a clerk in a bank. Baron had witnessed how life consistently beat his father down, especially as a man with no money. It was the reason his mother had left. Baron had vowed never to be at the mercy of any man or woman, and to do that, he needed money. Plenty of money. It was his personal golden rule.

He who has the gold, makes the rules.

"Shall we retire to the library?" Charles asked him.

"That would be fine," Baron replied. "Dinner was delightful, Mrs. Stanton. Thank you. Katherine, always a pleasure to see you."

Katherine pouted, clearly unhappy that he was leaving. She was the type of woman who would demand a great deal of his attention. She'd expect jewels and finery, of course. That much was expected, but she'd also want him to continue to woo her long after the vows. She was spoiled. The adored daughter of a wealthy and over-indulgent father.

He imagined Emily was nothing like her, but his opinion was based on nothing, really. He'd glimpsed Emily no more than a handful of times, watching her as she sat on the back porch of the mercantile. He'd had his men leave a table and two chairs for her. He'd spoken to her only once. She always wore the same muslin dress and yet, she carried herself with dignity, as though she'd been born for something quite different than the life of a shop girl.

Charles ushered him into his library. He offered him a drink. Baron shook his head.

"Coffee?" Charles asked.

"Thank you."

A servant was sent for coffee while the two men sat by the crackling blaze in the fireplace.

"I wondered if you'd given any thought to marriage," Charles asked.

Baron sighed. How many of his friends or acquaintances had started conversations in this exact way? They all had daughters, or sisters, or nieces who were delightful, beautiful, charming and sundry other wonderful things. The implication was clear. He should offer. Soon.

When he'd worked as a bounty hunter, men shielded their womenfolk from him. As he walked down the street, men pulled their wives and daughters aside to shield them from his rough ways. Rightly so. He'd been no more than a thug. His brutal ways had been a necessity.

Nowadays, Baron didn't have to beat men into submission, but sometimes it felt like it. The criminals he'd hunted were the kind of men who assaulted innocent women without remorse. Criminals always wanted more of what didn't belong to them.

Men of wealth were no better, at least not many of them. Many businessmen wanted a bigger piece of the pie, even if they hadn't worked for it. For that reason, he'd concluded long ago there was little difference between the steel magnate and a common cutthroat.

"Sometimes I think about taking a wife," Baron said. He looked down at his hands, rough from working the land, and so unlike Charles's hands or most men of wealth. "More lately."

His mind went to the girl with the sketch pad and the frightened look in her eyes. A girl who was unsuitable in every way. Too young. Too unfriendly. Too high-handed.

"You're thirty-two," Charles pointed out. "It's time to think about starting a family."

"It's true. It's time. Past time, some would say. I need a son to carry my name."

Charles nodded. "I wish I had a son of my own, but I hope to be blessed with a grandchild. I don't mean to offer my daughter as though I'm desperate, but Katherine is quite fond of you."

Baron suppressed a snort of derision. Charles was desperate, and Katherine didn't know the first thing about him. He thought about throwing that back at Charles, but recalled he wanted an invitation from the man. Diplomacy was a necessary evil. Instead, he offered a bland remark. "She's a lovely girl."

"I want you to know that she's refused other suitors in hopes that you'll..."

Charles's words faded. He took a swallow of his drink, keeping his gaze fixed on Baron. Baron gritted his teeth. He didn't want to hurt a young girl's feelings, but he didn't want to be held responsible for her refusing other young men.

Baron tried to choose his words carefully. "Katherine is a delightful young lady."

"But?"

"I'm not prepared to offer for any woman just yet."

And I'm in love with another...

The thought came from nowhere, unbidden. Baron grimaced. He felt something for Emily, there was no question about that. But love? That seemed unlikely. He was concerned about her, nothing more. His mind played tricks on him. Clearly. He pushed the thought aside, dismissing the idea out of hand. He was in love with no one, certainly not with an impossibly young girl who couldn't be bothered to engage in a simple conversation. He considered himself a thoughtful man. Practical. He didn't believe in love, certainly not love at first sight.

Charles got up from the chesterfield, set his drink on the mantle and went to a side table. Baron watched as he selected a cigar. The man peered at the box as if he were a medical doctor selecting a surgical instrument. Finally, he picked a cigar, sniffed it and set about preparing it.

"Katherine's very dear to me," Charles murmured.

"Of course."

"What would it take for you to make a decision?"

"A decision?"

"Selecting a wife, Baron. How can I make this more plain? I want to see Katherine settled. She won't have anyone but you. I have to think you've given her reason to believe you'd offer for her."

Baron leaned back and stretched his arm along the chesterfield. This wasn't the first time a friend or business acquaintance had tried to force his hand. It probably wouldn't be the last. Charles lit his cigar, glanced at him, and, seeing his expression, looked away.

"I haven't spent a single moment alone with Katherine," Baron said. "If she's led you to believe I offered for her, she's misspoken."

She was lying but Baron didn't want to use the word.

Charles pressed his lips together and turned away to face the fireplace. Baron tamped down his anger. He might be a ruthless businessman, one who would routinely crush competitors under his heel, but he was a man of his word. Always. Charles seemed to think he'd made an agreement when he hadn't.

"Baron," Charles said quietly. "I say this as a friend. Last month I had a small episode."

14

Baron waited, wondering what would follow. Some sort of heavy-handed appeal for him to make the offer for Katherine? A suggestion about religion, perhaps?

"Just a small scare – something with my heart. It's fine, but it made me realize life passes quickly," Charles said, tapping his ashes into the fireplace. "I only wish that I'd married earlier. Then maybe I might have been blessed with more."

"More?" Baron asked.

"More children. More years with my wife. More family time."

Baron got to his feet. He walked the length of the fine Persian rug, stopping in front of the window. "I don't need family time, Charles. I need a wife one day. A wife that keeps to herself and, God willing, a son to carry on my name. That's all."

Charles turned to face him. "You grew up without a mother. She left, for no good reason as I understand it, and you and your father had to manage without her, but that doesn't mean that all..."

"My mother has nothing to do with this. I hardly remember her. I'll get married one day to a woman who will give me what I need. A son. It should be easy enough. I won't let anyone strong-arm me into marriage."

Charles looked taken aback. "I offered a referral to the Presidio because I assumed you would take Katherine."

Baron slammed his fist against the bookcase. "I will not be coerced. Do you think you're the first man to offer me his daughter?"

Charles paled. Baron regretted his words immediately. Not because they were false. They were completely true, but still, he regretted his harsh tone. Charles had just admitted to being unwell. Baron knew he needed to rein in his temper. He didn't understand what had come over him.

The girl with the violet eyes. An image of her flashed in his mind. Ever since he'd first glimpsed her, she'd overturned his thoughts.

Baron raked his fingers through his hair. "I apologize, Charles. I'm not quite myself this evening. It's getting late. I'll see myself out. Please give my thanks to your wife and daughter."

Baron was through the door before Charles could respond.

Baron rode his bay gelding to the house of his sister and brother-in-law. Elizabeth and Henry lived beside the Methodist church where Henry worked as a minister. Riding down the quiet streets, he thought of Emily yet again. He should have been worried about Stanton's referral to the Cartel. Instead, he thought of *her*.

The quiet, aloof girl crept into his thoughts any time he had an idle moment. He resented how easily she'd taken over. The other day he'd actually spoken to her. He felt his lips curve into a smile as he pictured the way her lovely eyes had flashed with surprise and fury. She'd been angry with him, but her anger vanished when her aunt spoke to her. The way Emily dropped her gaze made something twist inside him. He'd wanted to snatch her away from the Nelsons, shield her from any threat or harsh word.

Later, he retired in his sister's guest room. He stood at the window, looked out into the inky darkness and felt a deep yearning well inside his chest. What was wrong with him? He never vied for the attention of a woman, never mind a mere girl. He could have any woman he wanted with the crook of his finger. With a growl of frustration, he'd turned in for the night, hoping for a reprieve from his preoccupation.

The next morning when he breakfasted with his sister and brother-in-law, the subject of marriage came up again. Not much of a surprise, really. Elizabeth dearly wanted him to marry so she could have a niece or nephew to make a fuss over. After twelve years of marriage his sister hadn't been blessed with children.

"How was Katherine?" she asked as she filled her teacup.

"Fine." Baron hoped that his terse reply would fend off too many questions.

"Henry and I were hoping for news of a proposal, weren't we, Henry?"

Baron's brother-in-law was deeply engrossed in the morning newspaper. He replied without looking up. "Yes, dear."

Elizabeth beamed at her husband and then turned her attention back to her brother. "Anything?"

"I didn't propose. I don't plan to anytime soon. I never said I intended to propose, Elizabeth."

His harsh tone was enough to make his brother-in-law glance up from his paper. Henry never did that. Baron gave him an apologetic shrug.

His sister pressed her lips together. "I see."

His sister was dear to him, and Henry had always been kind. When Baron first began studying at night, trying to improve himself, Henry offered encouragement. He'd sent Baron books on various topics. Those books, biographies, history books and anthologies, were the start of Baron's library. He treasured the gifts from Henry. Elizabeth and Henry were his only family, but lately Elizabeth had grown more insistent about him starting his own family.

A servant brought a basket of hot biscuits to the table, a platter of eggs and bacon, as well as an assortment of fresh fruit. Baron handed the platter of eggs to his sister who served herself as well as Henry. When she handed the plate back to Baron, she gave him a pointed look.

"I imagine the girl was terribly disappointed."

"It can't be helped. I'm too busy to court her properly. If she had expectations, that's her own doing. Or her parents."

Elizabeth shook her head. "Poor Baron, living all alone in that big house. I feel very sorry for you. A man shouldn't live alone, should he, Henry?"

"No, dear."

"I have just the idea," Elizabeth said, her eyes brightening. "Henry is taking a leave of absence from the church, a sabbatical. We should get word any day now. When we hear the news, we'll come to Magnolia for a visit."

Baron suppressed a groan. He loved his sister, but that didn't mean he didn't see right through her tactics. She'd campaigned for him to get married for the last year and a half, ever since she'd been told she couldn't have children. Elizabeth was kind and generous and a fine person, but patience was not one of her virtues.

"A visit. How nice. How long will you stay?" Baron asked, hoping he didn't sound as irritated as he felt.

Her eyes lit with amusement and she laughed – snickered really. Elizabeth Preston might be the dignified and pious wife of a Methodist minister. She might be as noble as the day was long, but Lizzy was his older sister. When their mother left, she took on the role of family matriarch. From an early age she'd practiced directing people, bossing them around. And she'd honed this talent on him.

To make matters worse she'd gone to a private girls' school on a scholarship. The years at St. Helen's had turned his sister into a formidable force when she wanted something, and she wanted him to have children. Sooner rather than later.

He saw the satisfied curve of her smile and knew he would be in for a miserable visit.

Henry didn't look up from his paper, but Baron was sure his brother-in-law had chuckled at his plight.

Chapter Three

Emily

Saturdays were always busy at the mercantile. By mid-day, Emily's body ached. Her stomach growled, but there was no help for it, the customers kept coming. They demanded their orders be filled. Even Carol and Roy looked weary, although Emily noticed that both had taken time to eat lunch, leaving her to tend to the throngs of customers clamoring for attention.

"Emily," Roy shouted. "Go to the storeroom and bring a bushel of apples."

She hurried to the back of the store and into the yard. The small storeroom sat behind the mercantile. Pushing the door open, she let her eyes adjust to the darkness. A noise caught her attention, mice scurrying under the floorboards most likely.

The baskets of apples sat on the top shelf. There was no stepladder that she could see, so she pushed a wooden chest under the shelves. Standing atop the chest, she could just reach the nearest basket. It was heavy and awkward. She nudged it closer to the edge and tried to grasp the sides to pull it down. The basket seemed to be caught on something. She gritted her teeth and pulled harder. The basket broke free and tumbled over the edge of the shelf, dumping the contents on her head. She fell off the chest and landed on the dusty planks of the floor.

Apples rolled across the floor. Closing her eyes, she groaned softly. Most, if not all, the apples would be bruised. With a sigh, she picked herself up and dusted her dress off. Sunlight spilled through the door casting bright light across the mess. Apples lay scattered everywhere. A pile sat in the middle of the storeroom. Others had rolled under shelves and cobwebbed corners.

She picked them up, one by one, and set them gently in the basket. The scent of apples filled the air, for some had fallen with such force, they'd split open. Apple pulp littered the floor. Later, she would try to steal away from her duties in the store to clean the mess.

After she'd picked up a dozen apples, the room darkened. She whirled around to see a man standing in the doorway, silhouetted against the afternoon sky. Fear coursed through her veins and rooted her feet to the floor.

He stepped forward. "Emily?"

The deep voice could only belong to Mr. Calhoun. For a moment, she couldn't think of what to say. She should tell him to leave. If Roy or Carol found her talking to him alone in a darkened storeroom, they'd assume the worst, of course.

"Are you hurt? I heard a woman's cry. I came as quickly as I could."

"Y-yes. I'm fine. Thank you."

He stepped inside and looked around the storeroom. Without a word, he knelt and began to pick up the apples. He moved around the small space, wordlessly retrieving fruit from dusty nooks and crannies. When he spied one behind a pallet of sugar, he heaved the pile of sacks aside, stooped to recover the apple, held it up for her inspection and smiled.

"I don't need your help," she blurted. "I don't want your help."

Ignoring her, he carried on with the task.

Inwardly, she cringed. Her words sounded colder than she'd meant, but she felt the sense of urgency grow. Mr. Calhoun needed to leave before Roy or Carol came looking for her.

"You shouldn't be here, Mr. Calhoun."

"A bushel of apples is too much for a little girl to carry."

"I'm not a little girl. I'm nineteen."

He rose, set his hand on his chest. "My apologies. I don't mean to suggest you're too young, just that you're too slight."

He teased her gently, but it surprised her. She couldn't decide if he was a nice person or not. On one hand he was helping her, but he had a forceful demeanor – the type of way that brooked no argument.

"Or," he mused, "maybe you're too young *and* too small."

She shook her head and set about the task of tidying the storeroom. The less said, the better. If she could get the apples inside, she'd try to explain what had happened to Carol. She'd offer to pay, of course. When the basket was filled, and every salvageable apple had been collected, she grasped a handle, intending to pick it up. Mr. Calhoun nudged her hand aside.

"Wait one second."

He reached up to the top shelf and pulled down a second basket of apples. He held it on his left shoulder, and then, with a quick motion, he swung the first basket from the floor up to his right shoulder, with one hand.

"Let's go." He left the storeroom.

Emily's heart sank. She hurried after him, almost forgetting to close the door behind her. By the time she'd caught up to him, he was halfway across the yard.

In the light of day, she could see that he wore work clothes, roughspun trousers and a linen shirt. She wondered what sort of work he did in addition to owning a great deal of property. He must have been working in the livery when he heard her shriek. She chided herself for being so foolish and drawing his attention. She certainly didn't want to meet up with him again. This was bad enough.

When they reached the door, she tried to stop him. "Mr. Calhoun, I only need one basket. You can set one down and give me the other. I can manage from here."

He stopped at the door and frowned at her. His eyes flashed, and she was certain she heard a low rumble coming from him.

"Open the door."

She did as she was told.

He gave a dismissive look and proceeded inside. He strode to the front of the store, his long legs closing the distance quickly. Emily had to run to keep up with him.

She heard Roy's voice first, a sort of surprised mutter when he saw Mr. Calhoun. She drew a sharp breath and braced herself for her uncle's outburst. He'd give her an earful if he knew all her misdeeds. She'd insulted the landlord. Ruined a bushel of apples. Taken too long. By the time everything was said and done, Roy would have a long list of wrongdoings.

The store was crowded, but the customers moved out of Mr. Calhoun's way. He was tall and powerful and commanded respect. The crowd parted, giving him a clear path to the counter. The customers who usually clamored the loudest stood silently as he stepped in front of them.

"Mr. Calhoun," Roy said, his gaze moving from the man before him to Emily and back again. "Is there a problem?"

"No problem at all," Mr. Calhoun replied evenly. He set the second basket down on the counter, the one that hadn't fallen.

A huff of relief came from Emily's lips. Carol, standing beside Roy, glared at her.

Mr. Calhoun went on. "I want to buy some apples, Roy. How much for this bushel," he asked, tilting his head to the basket on his shoulder.

Roy's eyes widened. "The whole bushel?"

"Come on, Roy. I don't have all day. I'm expecting a team of draft horses any minute."

"A dollar," Carol said, hurriedly.

Roy shot her a dark glare.

"Put it on my account." With that, he turned and walked out of the mercantile.

Emily stared after him. Her heart drummed against her ribs. She expected a reproach from Roy and Carol, but Roy said nothing and went back to helping a customer. Carol studied her for a moment and resumed her work as well.

Neither reproached her that evening either. Roy eyed her over a dinner they ate mostly in silence. Emily could see that he wondered just what the relationship between her and Mr. Calhoun might mean for him. She wanted to tell him there was nothing between them, but it was no use. He never believed a word she said. Any explanation always made his temper burn hotter.

At least tonight, he didn't have a glass of whisky in his hand.

Later that night, Emily lay in bed and thought about what Mr. Calhoun had done. It had been kind of him, for the apples were surely ruined, yet he'd paid for them anyway. Could he know how harshly Carol and Roy would have dealt with her?

She winced thinking that he felt sorry for her. She didn't want his charity.

Despite her exhaustion, she wrestled with how best to address the predicament. She could go to the livery tomorrow and pay him the money. Or she could forget about it and hope she never had to speak to him again. It pained her to think she was indebted to him. She fell asleep without resolving the dilemma. Her last thoughts before drifting off were of his broad shoulders and how he'd carried both heavy baskets as if they weighed nothing at all.

Chapter Four

Baron

The next morning Baron rose early. Despite the continued rain, he wanted to go to the livery to check on the team of draft horses he'd bought in Fort Worth. He had men who could do that sort of work for him, but he preferred to be the one buying horses and putting them through their paces.

He'd always had a feel for horses. Other animals too, but horses were especially important to him, and he felt he could read them. Since he first took over the livery, he'd tended to new horses in the first few days after they arrived.

His work in the livery was a welcome break from the tedium of banking. Time with the horses pleased him. Horses wanted nothing more than food, shelter and a kind touch. In return they gave their loyalty and hard work. The big draft horses were his favorite.

He arrived at the barn to find his stable hand, Jimmy, grooming the horses. The new horses, a matched pair of Clydesdales, stood in their stalls, eating their morning ration of grain.

"Someone took the new buggy?" he asked as he walked around the barn inspecting the horses one by one.

"Yes, sir," the stable hand answered. "Mr. and Mrs. Nelson took it to visit his brother."

Baron stopped and turned to face the young man. "Did they take their niece?"

Jimmy got a faraway look in his eye. He smiled wistfully. "You mean Emily?"

Baron frowned. "How many nieces do they have? Yes, I mean Emily."

Jimmy sobered. "Sorry, sir. No, they didn't take her. It was just the two of them, and then about twenty minutes later, Emily came by to ask if she could borrow a hammer."

"What does she need a hammer for?"

The young man shrugged. "I don't know, sir."

"Didn't you ask?"

"I did. She told me to mind my own business. That she'd have it back in an hour and that was all I needed to know."

Barron's lips quirked. He could well imagine Emily dismissing Jimmy just like she tried to dismiss him. He strolled to the back of the barn and surveyed the livery yard. The little storeroom where he'd found her yesterday amidst a spilled basket of apples was shut securely.

Rain fell steadily. He wondered what she needed a hammer for and decided that as the owner of the mercantile building he was within his rights to inquire. He crossed the barnyard and when he tried the handle of the back door, he found it open. Stepping inside, he heard the hammering. She worked on something upstairs.

If he went upstairs, he'd startle her. Emily was tough, stoic even, but she had a fragile side too. He'd seen that plainly.

The hammering paused. "Emily," he called out.

Her footsteps approached the stairwell, slowly, cautiously.

"It's Baron," he said, hoping to ease any worries she might have.

She descended the steps, the hammer in her hand. "Mr. Calhoun..."

He gestured towards the hammer. "What are you hammering?"

"A branch fell against a window upstairs. It must have happened sometime in the night. I'm trying to put a board over it, so the rain doesn't soak everything."

Her voice was softer than it had been yesterday or the first time he'd met her. Her hair hung loose past her shoulders. She wore the same, simple muslin dress. She looked young and vulnerable and he felt the absurd need to protect her from everything. Her aunt and uncle especially.

"Let me help you," he said, his voice gruff.

He half-expected her to brush off his offer, but she said nothing. Not that it would have mattered. He noted the difference in her response. He felt like he'd just won a competition... For the first time, he hadn't been dressed down by this scrap of a girl. It was ridiculous. Her acceptance felt like some sort of prize.

Taking the hammer from her, he went upstairs. She led him to the washroom beside the main bedroom. He glimpsed a pair of Roy's boots by the unmade bed. The upstairs of the mercantile didn't offer much in the way of living space. The prior tenant had been a bachelor.

"Where do you sleep?" he asked as he studied the broken window.

"In the little room under the stairs."

"That's hardly a bedroom."

"I won't be there long."

He turned to her in surprise. "Is that so?"

"I'm saving my money. I intend to leave Magnolia."

Leave Magnolia? He knew she'd only been in Magnolia a short while, perhaps a few weeks, but sometime after her arrival, he'd assumed she would be a permanent fixture in the town. Not here at the mercantile, but somewhere in town.

"Where are you going?" he demanded.

He waited for her to tell him that it was none of his concern, but she didn't. The hard look she always seemed to have softened. Her lips tilted almost imperceptibly.

"California," she said.

"What's in California?"

"The ocean," she said with a hint of impatience as if it were the most obvious thing in the world.

"Do you have family there? Friends?"

"No family, and no friends – yet."

He turned back to the broken window. She'd removed the broken glass and put it in a crate on the floor. A piece of wood leaned against the wall with nails hammered partway in. She'd done a good job so far, he had to admit. The area had been cleaned. The materials prepared. He was too irate to pay her a compliment.

"That's the most ridiculous thing I've ever heard," he grumbled.

"My apologies," she said.

He shot her an irritated look. Clearly, she was mocking him. She held her hand to her heart in the same way he had yesterday when he teased her about her youth.

"I suppose," she went on, her haughty tone seeping back into her voice, "that it's a good thing I'm not asking your permission, Mr. Calhoun."

He refused to dignify her sass with a reply. Instead he worked on the repair, making a note to order glass for the window. The tree outside would need to be trimmed too or else the new windowpanes would soon shatter with the next strong wind. He felt her eyes on him, the awareness of her attention warming his skin.

When he had the wood in place and the first few nails driven in, he glanced over his shoulder. Sure enough, she had her gaze fixed firmly on him. She startled when she realized she'd been caught staring, and she blushed furiously.

Her response made him smile. Maybe he'd won her over a tiny bit.

"When are the Nelsons due to return?" he asked.

"Not till tomorrow."

"You're here by yourself?"

"Yes, but it's fine. No one will bother me. I like it. Tomorrow I'll open the store by myself."

"That's a big responsibility for one person. I suppose they trust you."

"Not really. But I work for less than other people. Roy likes to grumble that I steal from the cash box."

He stepped back from the window and eyed his work.

"Why would he think that?"

"I worked as his bookkeeper. That was the agreement when they took me in. I made a mistake – or he claims I did. He accused me of cheating him."

His heart sank. Emily might be many things. Proud, and with what she said about California, probably impulsive, but he'd bet anything she was honest. And he was certain that Roy and Carol were mean, vindictive people. He clenched his fist, wishing he could find Roy right then and there and teach him a lesson or two.

If he could shield her from their harsh words, he would gladly do so.

"Come work for me," he said. The words were out of his mouth before he could stop them. "You can be my bookkeeper."

Her lips parted with surprise. He waited for her to reply with outrage. Instead, she grew solemn. "They wouldn't allow me to live here if I worked for you, Mr. Calhoun."

"I'll give you room and board."

She blinked and looked away. The pain in her eyes told him all he needed to know. He'd overstepped. She thought he meant something untoward. He blamed himself for his rash offer. He pounded the last nail into the board, hammering with more force than he needed. Stepping back, he surveyed the work. It would do for a few days.

"Thank you for your help," she said softly. "I have money in my room. I'd like to pay you for the apples."

He shook his head and turned to leave. She followed him down. With each step his regret over his suggestion grew. Emily had allowed him a glimpse into her life. He'd ruined it by offering what must sound like a scandalous arrangement. He could imagine what she thought – that he was an older man trying to compromise her virtue. She was beautiful, breathtaking. She was young, but even at her tender age, she'd probably suffered many inappropriate advances over the years.

Anger burned inside him, towards both himself and other men.

"Please let me pay you back," she said.

"It's not necessary, Emily. The horses eat the apples whether they're bruised or not."

"I don't wish to be beholden to you. Or any man."

There it was. Proof that a man had used her or tried to use her. He could hardly contain his fury. Stopping at the doorway, he tried to school his features to look indifferent.

"You're not beholden to me, Emily."

She gave him a skeptical look.

"I wanted the apples." He held up the hammer. "If you want to borrow a tool, I'll tell you right now, I don't lend them. But I will bring the tool and take care of any repair for you."

She nodded. "Thank you, Mr. Calhoun."

Silence stretched between them.

Mr. Calhoun... Everyone called him Mr. Calhoun. He disliked hearing the formality coming from her, and yet what did he want from the girl? An endearment? Hardly. Well, maybe. He liked to imagine her calling him by his given name, but now wasn't the time to press that issue. He offered a polite smile, allowed himself a last look into her startling eyes, and stepped out the door into the pouring rain.

Chapter Five

Emily

Roy and Carol returned from their visit with Roy's brother. For the next three weeks, they spoke of little else than the prospect of closing the mercantile and moving to East Texas to help run the family's lumberyard.

They had discussed this before. But now the conversations were far more energetic. How much happier they would be, back with family. And how Calhoun was unreasonable, and they'd be better off if they didn't have to deal with the like of him again.

Emily discovered that Roy had asked to buy the mercantile on numerous occasions. Baron had refused each time. Even when Roy offered twice his original offer, the answer was still no.

So, it was time to go, and Roy and Carol now just needed to convince themselves of that. And all Emily wanted was two more months.

With two more months, Emily would have enough for train fare. If she had to, she could manage sooner. She'd find a way. There was no way, though, she'd move to East Texas with her aunt and uncle.

She hadn't spoken to Mr. Calhoun since the day he'd helped her with the window. A time or two, she'd seen him in passing. He'd ignored her. He seemed to have forgotten all about her.

Sometimes, though, when Carol and Roy left for an overnight trip, she had the peculiar feeling that he took a special interest in the mercantile and the surrounding property. In the last moments of dusk, she'd see him leaning against the post in front of the livery. And in the first rays of dawn, she might see him patrolling the barnyard. She knew he was out there.

He never glanced her way, yet she could tell he was watchful. Did he stand guard? If so, did he want to protect her from an intruder or ruffian? The thought filled her with an odd mix of feelings. Part of her relished this notion and desperately wanted to believe it. The idea he might feel concern for her seemed precious to her. Men had watched her in the past, but never to keep her safe.

The other part of her wondered why she entertained such foolish notions to begin with. Baron Calhoun was a busy, powerful man. Why would he care about her?

She decided her imagination had gotten away from her and determined not to think about Baron Calhoun anymore. Instead, she tried to work hard in the store. She still harbored the faint hope that Roy and Carol might deem her efforts as helpful. She needed to know she was making a difference for them. Not that it mattered anymore. Once her uncle secured a new business, they'd be gone, and so would she.

They assumed she'd come with them. They never thought to ask her though. They were wrong. She'd part company from Roy and Carol and set out on her own. She might not have enough money to get to California, but she'd make her way west and at least she'd be a little closer.

One day, while working alone, a couple entered. The woman hurried to the counter where Emily worked, polishing silver spoons. Emily set the tarnished spoons aside and wiped her hands on a cloth.

"May I help you?"

"I certainly hope so," the woman said with a slight, but unmistakable, haughty air. "I can't imagine a small-town mercantile would have a watch band, but I suppose there's no harm asking."

The woman's husband wandered the length of the counter, humming softly under his breath. He seemed more amiable than his wife. When he glanced up, he stopped humming, smiled absent-mindedly, and promptly went back to perusing the displays.

The woman set a watch on the counter, a man's watch with a broken wrist band. "What sort of watch bands do you have, if any?"

Emily picked up the watch and studied it for a moment. "We have an assortment of leather bands." She directed her attention to the gentleman. "What color would you like, sir? The same brown?"

The woman waved her hand. "Brown would be fine, isn't that right, Henry?"

The man peered into a display case. "Yes, dear."

Emily presented the watch bands to the lady. When she'd picked a fine, dark leather band, Emily set about removing the old, broken band. She could feel the woman's eyes on her as she worked.

"You are a clever girl, aren't you? I assumed a gentleman would come to assist you. She's changing the band herself, Henry. Isn't that clever?"

"Yes, dear."

Emily smiled. "Yes, ma'am. I know how to fix watches too. I taught myself."

"An industrious girl," the woman marveled. She smiled approvingly. "And a pretty one, I might add. I've never seen a girl with eyes that color."

Emily blushed, keeping her gaze averted.

"Are you married?"

"No, ma'am."

The woman lowered her voice. "Any prospects?"

"No, ma'am."

The woman scoffed, good-naturedly. "I don't believe you. Surely, you're being modest."

Emily shook her head. "No prospects. My aunt wants me to offer to be a mail-order bride, but I don't intend to get married."

The woman let out an exasperated huff. "Young people these days. Why don't they want to get married? My brother refuses to marry as well. Even though he has a perfectly lovely sweetheart."

"Maybe she's not the right one."

"Of course, she's the right one. Rich. Beautiful. Refined. Baron doesn't realize what's plain as day. Isn't that right, Henry?"

A jolt of shock ran down Emily's spine. She kept her gaze on the watch, loosening the band with a small tool. Her skin prickled. Her heart thudded heavily.

He had a sweetheart...

With shaking hands, she finished attaching the band. Turmoil spun in her mind as she tried to make sense of what the woman said. Her chest burned with bitterness over the absurd thoughts she'd entertained about Baron. All along he had a girl – a sweetheart.

"I'm visiting Magnolia with the intention of seeing my brother married. Sooner rather than later. Maybe I'll do a little matchmaking for you while I'm here," the woman's smile widened. "I have quite a knack. My husband and I had intended to come for just a few days, but our home is having some repairs. We'll be here several weeks."

Before Emily could gather herself and reply, the woman called her husband over to try on the watch. The man shuffled to her side and the two talked about the watch and the band and the fit. Emily hardly heard what they said.

Baron had a sweetheart and she shouldn't care, but she did, to her surprise and dismay. She cringed inwardly at the memory of him standing outside his livery and how she'd imagined he watched over her. She was a fool. That much was certain. Shame scorched her heart.

"How much do we owe you, miss?"

"Fifteen cents," Emily said quietly.

The woman searched her purse for the money. The bell rang. Emily looked up to find Roy coming through the door. Carol followed a few steps behind. Emily hadn't expected them home till evening. Roy walked by, eyed the silver on the counter, his expression dark with anger. Carol looked flustered and Emily wondered what had happened on their latest trip.

"When you're done with that, get back to the silver," Roy barked. "Stupid is one thing, but lazy is even worse."

Baron's sister whirled to see who spoke. Emily's breath caught. She prayed the woman wouldn't say anything. Emily wasn't being lazy. She helped a customer, but Roy's outbursts never made sense. He got mad, because he was the type of person who was only happy *when* he was mad. That's how it seemed to her.

She'd grown used to Roy's outbursts but couldn't stand the idea of him treating Baron's sister rudely. Even though Emily would likely never see her again, it pained her to think of Roy insulting the lady.

But to Emily's surprise, it was the woman's quiet husband who spoke. "Now look here, young man."

Roy stopped in his tracks. Carol almost crashed into him. He turned slowly, his lips twisted into a sneer. "What?"

"This young lady has been an immense help. If she's behind in her tasks, it's because my wife and I have taken too much of her time."

Roy narrowed his eyes as if trying to place the man. Carol said a few words, urging Roy not to become angry. Henry closed the distance between himself and Roy. Dread coiled inside Emily's heart as she imagined Roy lashing out at the man. Maybe even physically. Roy wasn't afraid of any man, except for perhaps Baron Calhoun.

"Uncle Roy," she blurted. "This is Mr. Calhoun's sister and brother-in-law. They've come to town to visit him."

She watched as Roy grasped the meaning of her words. He nodded and rubbed his hand over his jaw. It seemed he was considering what to do next.

"I'll have the silver done in no time," she added. "I'm sorry it's taken me longer than it should have."

The woman gave a small hmpf.

"This young lady shouldn't be apologizing, sir." Her husband went on to say to Roy. "It is you who is in the wrong."

Emily winced. The man refused to back down. "It's fine. Really," she said quietly, praying he'd stop.

Roy turned his gaze to her. She saw his intent falter before he spoke, something she'd never witnessed before. "Emily," he said. "Finish the silver. When you can. Please."

She worried, wondering what would happen later when Roy decided to retaliate. She knew he'd blame her, of course. He'd imagine that she was the cause of the customer's dissatisfaction. She was certain it would all come back to an accusation of what she'd done or hadn't done.

What bothered her most wasn't Roy's retribution.

Baron Calhoun had a sweetheart.

A hollow feeling ached in her chest. Emily had imagined he cared about her. She'd been wrong.

Roy turned to leave, with Carol at his heels, casting furtive glances over her shoulder.

Henry straightened his jacket, fixing his gaze on Emily. "Be kind to one another, tenderhearted, forgiving one another as God in Christ forgave you."

His wife smiled at him.

Emily managed a small smile and spoke softly. "Ephesians 4:32."

He nodded.

"Thank you, sir," Emily said.

Suddenly she felt overcome with weariness. She saw the couple out the door, bid them good day and returned to her task of polishing the silver. Her mind turned over the sad news. She dwelt on it, unable to think of anything else. Of course, Baron Calhoun wooed a rich and beautiful girl. Why shouldn't he? He was handsome. He owned half the town. She'd allowed herself to indulge in girlish thoughts and wasn't that how rich, powerful men trapped young girls without means?

Never again, she reminded herself.

Chapter Six

Baron

Elizabeth had a list of grievances a mile long. The servants were using the wrong furniture polish. It left a foul odor in the air. The upstairs maid was impertinent. The roses needed pruning. Also, the tenant in the mercantile was rude.

He loved his sister, too much to remind her that they'd grown up living in a single-room garret.

"I think you should find a new tenant," Elizabeth advised as she nibbled her dessert.

They sat in the candlelit dining room, finishing dinner. The church rectory needed a new roof along with some repairs. Instead of coming for just a few days, Henry and Elizabeth would be with him the better part of a month. This was the first of what would be several weeks' worth of dinners, he realized. If each dinner was filled with advice, he might start counting them down. But the last comment caught his attention.

"What's that about the mercantile?"

"The owner is a horrid, horrid man."

Baron glanced at his brother-in-law. Henry gave no clue about Elizabeth's assertion. He was too busy helping himself to another slice of cake.

"He insulted the shop girl," Elizabeth said. "He called her stupid and lazy."

A rush of anger surged through him. The words darkened his thoughts. He fought the urge to leave the table, depart the house and ride into town to confront Roy Nelson. How he despised the man. He'd never cared for him, but now, hearing that Roy insulted her, and thinking how Emily suffered living there, he'd like nothing better than to beat him senseless.

"And then, my Henry told him he mustn't speak to her that way. The girl had been helping us with Henry's watch, after all. We'd taken her away from her chores. Henry called him out on his beastly behavior." Elizabeth gave her husband an adoring look. "I was so proud of my brave Henry."

Henry chuckled, his face coloring.

"The shop girl is such a lovely thing, too," Elizabeth said. "Young and far too delicate to receive such a rude reprimand. She seemed so out of place working in a mercantile."

Anger twisted inside him. "I know of the girl."

"Her eyes are the color of violets."

"I know," he growled.

He'd thought of Emily night and day for the last three weeks. While he should have been traveling to visit the mines in the hill country, he'd remained in Magnolia. The nights when he knew she was alone in the store, he'd prowled around the property to make sure there were no evil-doers lurking in the shadows, scoundrels thinking of ways to do her harm. He *knew* she was beautiful. Her steely nature, her infuriating stubbornness and her breathtaking loveliness had been a pure, unrelenting torment.

Later that night, he bid Elizabeth and Henry a good night. Instead of retiring, he went to the barn, saddled his horse and rode the five miles into Magnolia. The livery was quiet. His night watchman met him at the door and took his horse. Baron went to the back of the barn and scanned the mercantile.

The moonlight lit the building with a silvery glow. His breath caught in his throat when he spied her. She sat at the table on the porch. A lamp burned, casting a pool of light around her as she read a book. Unable to stop himself, he crossed the barnyard, as if directed by an uncontrollable need to make sure she was well.

The last time he'd found her here, she'd been drawing. He'd startled her. This time she heard him. Lifting her gaze to meet his, she appraised him thoughtfully.

"Mr. Calhoun," she said evenly.

She wore the same muslin dress. Her hair hung down, a silken swath that made him wonder what it would feel like between his fingers. He stopped a few paces from the porch.

"Emily," he said. "I understand that Roy Nelson spoke unkindly to you today."

A look of vulnerability flashed behind her eyes. His heart squeezed with pain. How often did Roy Nelson abuse his niece? Daily?

"It was nothing. I'd neglected my duties, but I finished everything a half-hour ago."

"If you married, you'd escape this..." His words faded as he gestured towards the mercantile.

He couldn't say the words he wanted to say. *If you married me, you'd escape this.*

She shook her head. "I refuse to marry."

"Why is that?" he snapped. "Never been in love? Of course, you haven't, you're scarcely more than a child."

She recoiled but recovered quickly. "No, I haven't been in love. Not like *you*."

She practically spat the words. He wondered what the hell she meant, but didn't ask. Why bother? She wouldn't give him a straight answer.

He drew closer. Glancing at the book on the table, he decided a change of subject was in order. "What are you reading?"

"A book about clocks and watches."

She hadn't snapped at him. This was progress.

"That's interesting."

He thought it sounded about as interesting as watching grass grow, but more than anything he wanted to talk with her. Making conversation wasn't his strong suit.

She gave a sheepish smile. "The prior tenant left a number of manuals in the storeroom. I'm trying to better myself. Learn new things."

A slow blush bloomed across her skin. He wondered if her skin was as soft as it looked.

"I'm sure it sounds ridiculous," she murmured.

"I don't think so. I like to better myself too."

She smiled at him and the way it transformed her face stole his breath. Elizabeth was wrong. Emily wasn't merely lovely. The word didn't do her justice. Emily was far more than lovely. She was ethereal. Beauty without equal.

"I found some broken clocks in the storeroom and I've tried to fix them," she said. "I've had some luck, but..."

His heart warmed to hear her words. She was showing a small part of herself again. He craved more. He relished the way she spoke to him in such an unguarded way.

"But?" he prompted.

"I'm having trouble with one of the clocks."

"What sort of trouble?"

"I've worked on it, and it runs now. But it runs backwards."

He chuckled.

She tried to look stern, but he saw the way her lips quirked as she suppressed her laughter.

"Backwards? There are some that might want a clock to run backwards," he said.

She searched his eyes for a long moment. "Would you?"

"Never."

"I wouldn't either. I just want time to go forwards. It's better that way." She smiled awkwardly. "Not that we have a choice, of course."

Her smile made a rush of happiness flow through him. He was transfixed, staring like a fool. She blushed at the attention. He forced his gaze away from her, glanced up at the top level of the house wondering if Roy and Carol had gone to sleep. He hoped so, for Emily's sake.

"Emily, I know you want to travel west. Why don't you let me give you the money? I'd happily pay your train fare. I'd even escort you out there and make certain you had a home. That you were safe and well-cared-for."

Her face fell. She took a sharp breath as her hand fluttered to her throat. A small sound of dismay came from her lips.

"Just to make sure no one troubled you, Emily." He offered his explanation. "That's all. We would travel separately, of course."

She got to her feet. "I wouldn't want you to go through the trouble, Mr. Calhoun."

"Emily," he said sharply, his anger sparking. "Why do you have to be so proud? I want to help you. I'm trying to make things better for you."

She picked up her book and the lamp and turned to the door. "I don't want your help, Mr. Calhoun. I don't want anything from you."

With that she stepped inside the mercantile and shut the door firmly behind her.

Baron stared at the door that had just been shut in his face. For a moment, he indulged his imagination. He thought about storming inside, picking up Emily and carrying her off. The urge grew. He could simply pluck the stubborn girl from danger. And then what? Take her someplace safe, of course, but then she would forever regard him with the same mix of fear and contempt she ofttimes showed now.

"Emily," he whispered. "I'd do anything for you."

He waited, like a fool, half-expecting an answer, but the only reply came from a barn owl nesting in the livery. With a low growl, he turned away. Later, as he rode home, he wondered how he might get Roy's help with settling the girl somewhere safe. The man was as driven by money as Baron was. Perhaps he could pay him off, perhaps sell him the mercantile in exchange for Emily.

The idea struck him like a thunderbolt, stealing his breath. Offer the mercantile for Emily... if he saw the notion through, he would essentially be bartering for a woman. The idea was outrageous, but he didn't care. Other than a few expensive gifts for Elizabeth and Henry, Baron had never given anything to anyone.

For Emily, he was ready to pay any price to get what he wanted more than anything in the world – to protect her.

Chapter Seven

Emily

The first time Roy didn't pay her wages, he promised to give her double the following week. That week came and went, and he announced he needed to hold the money for her room and board. He told her after dinner, in their small kitchen upstairs. Emily looked to Carol, but her aunt kept her gaze averted.

"You ain't worth anything in the store anyway," he said, his words slurring. "I can't get an honest day's work out of you, so why should I pay you?"

"I'm in the store each morning before you or Carol," she countered.

"You think I don't know about your little plans to go to California? What you going to do there? Whore like your mama?"

Emily recoiled. Her eyes stung. She wanted to hurl insults back at him but knew she'd be out on the street the instant she did. Instead, she held back, tucking her words away for one day when she could simply walk out the door. She said a quiet thank you for dinner and excused herself.

"What about the dishes?" Roy yelled.

"I'll do them shortly." She hurried downstairs to her room and pulled out the bottom drawer. Searching the back corner, she ran her fingers along the edges but found nothing. Her money was gone. A noise behind her drew her attention. Carol stood in the doorway.

"I know you want to leave us," she said quietly. "Might be for the best. Roy keeps looking at you in a way that I don't care for."

"Aunt Carol, I was saving money for a train ticket."

"What are you going to do out there with no husband?"

"I don't know exactly. I can work. I *like* to work."

"I know you don't want to marry, but you need to think that over. Last week, me and Roy were in Temple. I came across a notice in the paper. Men looking for mail-order brides."

Emily let out a sound of disgust. This topic always made her sick to her stomach. "I would never stoop that low. Marry a stranger. Not in a hundred years."

Carol scowled. She pulled a newspaper clipping from her pocket and unfolded it. "Look. This would be perfect for you."

Emily was certain it would not be perfect but couldn't stop herself from reaching for the clipping. The torn page held a number of requests for mail-order brides. One was circled. Emily read the words.

Companion and wife wanted. Older, wealthy gentleman seeks bride to come to San Francisco.

"When I read that, I just knew that the good Lord meant for you to write him, Emily."

Slowly the truth dawned to Emily. She could see it clearly. With a gasp of anguish, she lifted her hand to her lips. "You told Roy to stop paying me, didn't you? And then you took the money I'd been saving."

"I take no pleasure in any of this, but I won't stand back and watch you ruin your life. You need to find a husband. You can't have mine."

Emily sank to her bed, too distraught to reply.

Carol pressed her lips together. "I'm sure you won't believe me, but I care about you. You're my only kin. I don't approve of what my sister did or how she led her life. I don't want you to go down the same path. Don't you see? Without a man, how will you get by?"

Emily had no answer for her aunt. Ever since she'd arrived in Magnolia, she'd thought only of leaving for the west. Much as she hated to admit it, Carol was right. She'd been so caught up in thoughts of escape she hadn't made proper plans.

"An older man might not even be interested in relations," Carol said softly.

Emily flinched at the thought. She'd heard enough of her mother entertaining her "gentleman callers." The memory of the men, and the way they'd given her filthy, appraising looks as they left, sent a shudder down her spine.

Carol set a sheet of paper on the bedside table along with a pen. "Roy doesn't know anything about the money you were hiding in your bottom drawer. You write a letter to this gentleman, and I won't say a word."

Emily stared at the pen and paper. Her hopes faded away as she sat on her bed, holding the advertisement. A mail-order bride. How could she possibly endure marriage to a complete stranger?

"You take care of that letter, and I'll tidy the kitchen," Carol said. "Tomorrow, we'll take it to the post office together."

As much as Emily hated the idea of writing the letter, she knew she had no choice. Carol held her future in her cold hands. She couldn't stay with Carol and Roy. She couldn't stay in Magnolia, not if it meant watching Baron Calhoun marry his sweetheart.

That evening, Emily went to the little table on the back porch. By the light of the lamp, she wrote a letter to Mr. Edward Tully. She wrote a few lines about her varied interests, and a few more about her appearance. This was the part of the letter that made her cringe.

Some men find me pleasing.

It was true, some men did find her pleasing, but she found no joy in their attention. If anything, she discouraged their admiration. There was only one man whose approval she craved, but he loved another. Bitterness burned inside her as she wrote her final lines to Mr. Tully.

When she was done, she went inside to fetch an envelope. The store was in shadows and quiet. The only sound came from upstairs, as Carol washed the dishes. Roy probably snored in his chair. She felt her way along the back counter to the area where they stored stationery. Ever since she began work at the mercantile, she'd always paid for anything she took from the store, but tonight she was in a reckless mood. Not only that, but now she had no money.

She found an envelope and returned to her table on the porch but found her letter was no longer on the table. The lamp flickered, casting shadows over the surface of the table. The pen lay where she left it, but no letter. A light breeze blew. She searched the area with hopes that it lay nearby.

A voice from the shadows startled her. "Did you lose something?"

From the darkness a shape appeared. Baron Calhoun held her letter. He offered it to her, a smile playing on his lips. She snatched the letter from him, but to her horror, he also held the newspaper clipping.

"Seems your plans have changed," he drawled.

"It's none of your concern," she snapped. "Give me the advert back."

He waved it in the air, taunting her. "Sending a letter to the elderly suitor? Good idea. Maybe he'll have the good manners to die right after the vows."

She seethed but managed to tamp down her anger. Now was not the time to lash out at him, certainly not until she had the paper back. Coaxing a smile to her lips, she proceeded with as much courtesy as she could muster.

"My aunt has requested I write to this gentleman. She's concerned about me traveling alone to California. She also thinks I'm a harlot and that I have designs on her husband."

The words tumbled out. Emily wished she hadn't said them but was too tired to care about what he thought. She'd hoped he might show a shred of compassion or dismay. Instead, he chuckled.

"Emily, you couldn't possibly be a harlot. A good harlot needs to enjoy flirting, or at least a little conversation with men. You realize that, don't you?"

"You know about these things?"

"Not personally."

"Never consorted with a harlot?"

"I'm a stingy man."

"A fine man like you probably doesn't need to pay for a woman's attention."

She'd never said anything so coarse in her life.

He laughed. His amusement made the last vestiges of restraint fall away. Fury burned inside her. She tried to grab the advertisement, but he held it out of her reach. He grinned as he backed away from her.

"Mr. Calhoun," she said softly as she stalked across the barnyard, trying to get closer to him.

"Yes, Emily."

He stopped and waited. The dark made it impossible to see his expression, but she knew with complete certainty that he still grinned at her.

"Is this how you treat your sweetheart?" she demanded. "By teasing and mocking her."

"I don't have a sweetheart."

She scoffed. "Of course, you don't."

He grunted and offered her the newspaper back. "I don't have a sweetheart. Take your advert, but don't write that man. He doesn't deserve you."

"The man just wants a companion."

"I'd like a companion too."

His voice was gruff, and the tone bordered on indecent. Any minute he'd propose an arrangement, offer to keep her comfortably in exchange for the privilege of visiting her two or three times a week. Always in the evening. Or perhaps in the morning before lunch. She'd heard these types of negotiations before.

The thought that Mr. Calhoun would offer some sordid arrangement twisted her heart. Part of her still wanted to believe he cared for her. She was leaving. Soon. And she wanted to remember him in that way.

"Good night, Mr. Calhoun." Her voice shook. She prayed he'd leave her alone and let her return to the mercantile without further talk. He didn't follow her, thank goodness.

Stepping inside the store, she came face to face with Roy. He leaned against the wall, his arms folded. Rage burned in his eyes. "Who were you talking to out there?"

Her thoughts swirled. She couldn't imagine what to say. Clearly, he'd heard parts of the conversation, but if she told him it was Mr. Calhoun, a man Roy disliked intensely, things could go from bad to worse. And yet, if he found her in a lie, she'd have little recourse. He'd accuse her of lying about other things.

Roy's hand shot out so fast, she didn't have time to respond. He struck her across the face. The impact drew a cry from her lips. She staggered back and fell to the floor. Roy loomed over her.

"It was Mr. Calhoun," she whispered. "He wanted to know if I was all right."

Roy shook his head. "You letting him have his way with you?"

"No."

He grunted. "Next time I see him, I'll ask what you two were talking about."

She remained quiet, hoping he'd leave her in peace.

"Baron Calhoun's the last man you want to whore around with. He'd chew you up and spit you out. Cheap floozy like you."

For a long moment, Roy didn't move. Finally, he turned away. Emily listened as his heavy footsteps echoed up the stairs and as he crossed the room overhead. Roy went to his room and spoke a few harsh words to Carol.

Emily pulled herself to a sitting position, trying to collect herself until finally she found the will to get up. She gathered the paper and pen, went into her room, then lit the lamp and studied her reflection, wondering if she'd bruise. Likely. There was already a welt, but maybe the bruise would fade before she met Mr. Edward Tully.

Chapter Eight

Baron

Baron frowned at the waterwheel as it spun slowly. The rains of a few weeks ago had replenished the rivers, but it hadn't been enough to keep the wheel moving properly. The mill couldn't keep up with demand at this rate. He already had unhappy and impatient customers. He rubbed his jaw as he walked along the riverbank.

"A bigger wheel," he muttered.

He strolled up the path and went inside the mill. Phillip, the caretaker, startled when he saw him. Baron sighed, wondering why his workers always acted fearful around him. He rarely got angry with them or lost his temper, so why did they all recoil?

"We need a bigger wheel, Phillip. The diameter should be increased to twenty-two feet."

"Y-yes, sir."

Baron frowned. "You feeling all right?"

"Just fine."

"All right. Send me word on how quickly the new wheel can be built and put in place. And... you're doing a good job here. Why don't you take the afternoon off?"

The man blinked. "You're letting me go?"

"Did I say that?"

"No, sir, but I've worked here ten years and you've never given me an afternoon off."

Baron shrugged. "There's probably not much you can do with the river so low."

He left without another word. Heading toward the mercantile, he whistled, thinking about Emily. He hadn't slept all night. Despite that, he was in fine spirits. He intended to make Roy an offer he couldn't refuse. He'd not only give him the mercantile, he'd forgive the loan Roy had taken to start his business. In exchange, he'd demand Roy's permission to marry Emily. He didn't like giving Roy anything, but came to the realization sometime around dawn that he'd pay any price.

Over breakfast, he'd told Elizabeth and Henry that he intended to court a young lady in town. Both of them had stared at him with complete bewilderment as if the idea was too astonishing for them to comprehend. He smiled, thinking about their shocked expressions. Everyone would be shocked, probably his lawyer most of all. Stanton had all but assumed Baron would offer for Katherine. The situation couldn't be helped.

Baron had made up his mind. Emily might not care for him, but she desired him. He was certain. And he knew he desired her. Not so long ago, he'd only wanted a wife to give him an heir. Now he imagined so much more. A wife and family. He'd do everything he could to woo and charm Emily. Eventually, she'd grow to love him.

He entered the mercantile and smiled when he saw that it was empty except for Emily. She stood at the counter, taking an inventory of kitchen spices. When he closed the door, the bell rang. She looked up. The sound of the bell faded. He heard her take a sharp breath.

At that precise moment, he saw the bruise.

Her eyes widened, and she turned away. With her back to him, she bowed her head with what he knew was shame. Her shoulders hunched.

Anger surged through him. Roy had hit her. Or was it Carol? It didn't matter.

Leaning against the door, he reached back and drew the latch to lock the door. Customers might expect to enter the store, but he didn't want anyone to see Emily. Not like this.

All his plans faded from his mind. The mercantile. Roy. Offering for Emily. No, he wouldn't offer anything to Roy Nelson. He'd simply take her. It was what needed to be done.

"You're coming with me, Emily."

She turned. Keeping her gaze averted, she handed him an envelope. "Roy's upstairs. He wanted me to give you the money for this month's rent."

"I'm not leaving without you."

"I can't. I won't. I have reasons that I can't tell you about."

He took the envelope and tapped it against the counter. "Are you married?"

She lifted her gaze to meet his. "Of course not."

The plum-colored bruise ran the length of her jaw. Emily, *his* Emily, had a welt on her face, the lower edge a clear outline of a man's palm. Dark rage clouded his vision.

"If you're not married, you're free to be with me."

Behind him, someone knocked on the door. She cast a worried look at the door and lifted her gaze to his. She looked at him pleadingly, silently imploring him to let her open the door.

"I shouldn't be alone with you, Mr. Calhoun," she whispered. "Please just take the money and leave me be."

Suddenly, he recalled the envelope. He opened it and stared. The envelope was empty. He showed her. "Where's the money?"

With a trembling hand, she reached for the envelope. She opened it and stared. "I saw him put the money in there. Forty dollars. He counted it out."

"I'm sure it's just a mix-up. I'll ask, Roy. I need to have a talk with him anyway."

More knocking came from the locked door. Roy bellowed from the rooms upstairs. His footsteps drew nearer as he descended the steps.

"Please go," she whispered.

"You're coming with me, Emily. Today. Now."

Her eyes filled with tears. "I can't."

Roy stormed into the storeroom. "Why in the hell..."

His words faded when he saw Baron.

"Mr. Calhoun," he muttered. He glanced at Emily. "Everything all right?"

Baron bit back his rage. "Everything's fine. I've come to ask for Emily's hand in marriage."

Roy's mouth gaped like a gaffed catfish. After a moment, he snapped it shut. "The hell?"

Baron kept his gaze on Roy but spoke to Emily. "Gather what you need."

"You can't take her," Roy snarled. "She works for me."

"Not anymore." Baron moved closer to Roy.

Emily hurried away.

"She's a whore just like her mother," Roy said under his breath.

Baron grabbed him by his shirt and slammed him against the wall. "You're lucky she went to her room and didn't hear you call her that."

Roy tried to pry Baron's fingers from his shirt. Baron smashed him against the wall again.

"You'll never hurt Emily again. Pack up your things. Leave Magnolia. Consider this an eviction notice."

"You can't evict me from Magnolia." Roy's face was crimson from sheer rage. He tried to push Baron away, but Baron's grip was too tight. "What about my store? My goods?"

"Everything's mine."

Roy stared at him, his expression somewhere between fury and disbelief. "The loan...?"

"That's right."

"You can't do that," Roy sputtered.

"I can. I will." Baron pinned him to the wall and snarled his final warning. "If I ever see your face in this town, I'll kill you."

Chapter Nine

Emily

Sitting in her cramped room, Emily listened to the sounds of Carol and Roy packing their belongings. Their footsteps crossed the upstairs floorboards, the sound echoing across the ceiling of her room. Baron directed his men to load things onto a buckboard outside. His was the only voice she heard. Carol and Roy had been cowed into silence by Baron's fury.

People went up and down the steps, carrying or dragging Carol and Roy's possessions.

With each passing moment, her dread grew, a heavy weight inside her. Once before, she'd known the same terrible helplessness. It began when her mother died, leaving her in the care of a stranger. Orson Whittier, a wealthy shipping merchant, had paid for the last few years of her schooling. Emily discovered the written agreement among her mother's papers. The understanding was that Emily would be his when she came of age. It also included a tidy sum to be paid to Emily's mother each year, as custodian of "his investment."

Her mother had sold her.

Emily had no money, but she didn't allow that to stop her from doing what she needed to do. She sold off her mother's possessions – her furniture, paintings, rugs. All of it, sent to auction. She used the money to pay her mother's debts, but more importantly, Emily hired a Pinkerton man to find out everything there was to know about her benefactor. A month after her mother's funeral, Mr. Whittier arrived, intent on collecting his investment.

He hadn't expected that she waited for him. And she was ready.

She recalled Mr. Whittier's startled expression. He stood in the middle of the empty apartment, probably wondering what had happened to all the furniture. Emily didn't bother to explain. Instead, she read him a list of his family members, including his wife. Then she went on to list his business associates. All of them would receive a letter from her, detailing the shameful agreement he'd made when Emily was no more than a young girl.

Her Pinkerton agent had kindly stayed on for one final task, to escort the astonished Mr. Whittier from the apartment. Amid Emily's grief, she had one shining moment of triumph. Sometimes she'd think back on that afternoon and the way Mr. Whittier had grown pale, and then crimson with red-hot indignation. The memory always made her smile.

Baron Calhoun was no Orson Whittier.

No. If anything, he'd approve of her trying to outwit him. He'd be amused and probably see it as a game of cat and mouse.

As the sounds faded and then stopped, Emily realized her aunt and uncle had left. They hadn't said good-bye. Perhaps that was for the best. They were gone. Her only family members. It dawned on her that she'd likely never see them again.

She waited, her heart in her throat. Her hands felt clammy. She wiped them on the silken fabric of her dress, not caring if she ruined the expensive frock. Footsteps broke the silence. Sitting with her back to the door, she turned to look over her shoulder. Baron appeared tall, and broad-shouldered, nothing like any banker she'd ever known. The gentlemen her mother called her "special friends" were short, squat men with soft, milky hands. Baron set his work-roughened hands on the doorframe, regarding her for a long moment.

"I would bargain with you if I could," she said.

"There's nothing to bargain for."

"Even if there were, I probably wouldn't manage to convince you." She rose, turning to face him. She trembled as she braced herself for his response. "I'm not skilled at charm or persuasion."

His gaze drifted over her, but his expression was more one of surprise than desire. She'd never wanted to please a man before, but she needed to please Baron, and for that reason, she'd donned one of the dresses her mother had made for her. She'd offer him what he wanted. And then he'd be done with her. She'd have her bargaining chip to leave Magnolia.

He drew close, stopping a pace from her. "You are so lovely, Emily."

Her breath caught. He'd told her what she hoped to hear, yet his voice was edged with sadness. In the dim light of her room, she saw the regret in his eyes. A horrifying thought flashed in her mind, that he might reject her. That she wasn't lovely *enough*.

"Men would kill for a woman like you," he said. "I know I would."

She waited for him to continue, sensing a dismissal. If she'd been ashamed to wear the dress, she'd felt it a thousand-fold now. Baron didn't want her after all.

"I care for you, Emily."

"But?" she whispered.

"There's no '*but*'. We'll wed just as soon as my brother-in-law will marry us. And one day, we'll be man and wife in the truest sense. I wouldn't take a bruised, frightened girl to our marriage bed."

"You want to marry... *me*?"

The corners of his lips twitched. "How many times do I have to ask?"

"I don't believe you."

"You don't have to. You'll see soon enough. Finish packing your things and change out of that dress. I don't want anyone to see you like that."

Chapter Ten

Baron

Baron ordered the store's sign taken down. He didn't want Roy Nelson's name hanging on the front of the building for a moment longer than necessary. Immediately the town buzzed with the news. Three different men approached him about taking over the reins of the store.

Even before Roy and Carol had the last of their belongings packed, Baron had made a verbal agreement with new tenants. With a handshake he transferred ownership to a young couple from Alsace-Lorraine. They'd inquired about the mercantile before and owned a small bakery in town. Baron felt certain they would be excellent tenants.

Returning to the store, Baron found Emily in her room, her trunks packed. She wore her muslin dress, thankfully. A flicker of irritation flared inside his thoughts. She'd been a vision in the silk dress. An indecent vision. He didn't want other men seeing her dressed like that. Roy had called her a whore and her mother too, but Baron didn't care about her past.

"Are you ready, Emily?"

She nodded, eyeing him warily. He ushered her out of her bedroom, and as they walked out the back door, he offered his arm.

Her lips parted with surprise. "Everyone will see."

"That's what I want. To show the world."

Letting her gaze drift to his arm and back to his eyes, she stood, rooted to the spot. "I've never held a man's arm."

Her blush deepened.

"I would be honored if you would take my arm."

Slowly, she lifted her hand and set it in the crook of his arm. Her touch was feather-soft. It hit him with the force of a brawler's fist, knocking his thoughts clean from his mind. His chest tightened. His breath felt ragged. His brow dampened.

Emily looked dismayed. "Are you all right, Mr. Calhoun?"

"Of course. I'm fine. Stop calling me Mr. Calhoun."

He willed his feet to move towards the barn. Trying to ignore the feel of her hand, he tried to think of something interesting or endearing to say to her. They'd have a thirty-minute drive on the buckboard. He was eager to talk with her, to know her better. Normally, he merely tolerated women's company. Even Elizabeth could ramble on about dull topics, trying his patience. He knew Emily would fascinate him. He hoped she might grow to find him interesting as well.

A small murmur of pleasure came from her lips. He followed her gaze to where the new horses, the matched pair of draft horses, stood in the barnyard. His men had harnessed them to one of his better wagons.

"Are those animals yours, Mr. Calhoun?"

He wanted to chide her for calling him by his formal name, but the look on her face pleased him so well, he set the comment aside. Her eyes sparked with admiration as she looked at the new horses. Even her lips, curved slightly, seemed to hint at a smile.

"They are mine. I bought them in Fort Worth."

They drew closer. Emily pulled her hand from his arm. Immediately, he missed her touch, but he couldn't help smiling as she moved to horses and stroked their noses.

"I love all animals. But horses are my favorite."

"I agree."

Her eyes held a slightly dazed expression. Her voice sounded small. She had to be in shock over the day's events, as was he.

"My mother sent me to a very good school," she said quietly. "I did well in math and science. There was a time when I imagined studying to become a veterinary doctor."

Her eyes still held a faraway look but they shone with pleasure. He held his breath, wondering if she would share more of herself. She wanted to care for animals. He could hardly imagine her, with her narrow shoulders and slight frame, wrangling a sick calf, or delivering a foal.

She frowned. "You think that's amusing?"

"Not at all," he said. "I know you're very bright. But the men I know who doctor animals are all big, strong men."

"Well, even if I found a university that would admit a woman, and if I had a way to pay for my schooling, I could never have managed."

"Because you're so slight?"

Her frown deepened. "No. I'm not slight. I'm very strong, but I can't stand the sight of blood."

He schooled his features to keep from smiling. Not that he found her words humorous, but he was pleased she'd told him about herself. It felt like a small gift. One he hadn't expected, which was always the best kind.

She leaned forward, as if sharing a secret. "I faint."

He lowered his voice. "That would be a problem."

She shook her head and turned away. The moment was over, yet it filled him with the furtive hope that she might confide in him more. Soon.

Baron ordered two of his men to bring Emily's trunks from the small room in the mercantile. When they were loaded on the wagon, he helped her up. He climbed up to sit beside her and gathered the reins. Snapping them, he urged the horses into a trot. They drove together, through the town of Magnolia and climbed the road to his home.

She sat beside him, looking more like a lovely duchess than a drab shop girl. Her skin, fair and smooth, was a stark contrast to her dark hair. Her long lashes accentuated her lovely eyes. Her carriage was proud without being haughty.

His gaze drifted to her modest dress. He tried to push the memory of the revealing dress she'd worn earlier that day. He needed to show he was a gentleman, even though he'd railroaded her into coming with him to his home to marry him.

Chapter Eleven

Emily

Baron's home sat on a ridge overlooking Magnolia. Constructed of massive blocks of limestone, the proportions reminded her more of a castle than a Texas ranch house. A veranda wrapped around the first floor. On the second floor, a terrace overlooked a flower garden, brimming with tulips.

Some distance from the house stood a barn. Cowboys worked in a distant corral. Dust billowed in the air and calves bawled.

"I own ten thousand acres."

His tone held a note of arrogance. She nodded, unsure what to say. Ranches in Texas were known for being large, and men prided themselves on having vast tracts of land.

She took in the rolling fields, the groves of oaks and the animals grazing. It was clear why he was proud of his land. "It's very pretty," she said quietly.

A faint breeze blew around the grand home, carrying the smell of wood smoke. The aroma of food was faint but made her stomach rumble. Flower pots flanked the door, bright blooms cascading over their edge and offering a quaint, inviting picture. The house was elegant, yet cozy, or so it seemed to her. She was overcome with the desire to push through the door and wander the rooms of Baron's home. She wanted to know more of him, to see how he lived and imagine how she might fit into his life.

The notion stirred a deep longing inside her. She'd never dared hope for anything like this and the yearning frightened her. Why wish for the impossible?

A man and woman appeared in the door. They waved and descended the stone steps. As they drew near, Emily saw that it was Henry and Elizabeth, the couple from the mercantile who tried to defend her. Emily recoiled when she saw their expressions of dismay. They'd see her face and her bruises. Shame twisted inside her.

"Emily, my dear," Elizabeth said, recovering quickly. "Baron told us he intended to bring you."

"We're glad to see you," Henry added. His brow knit. He sounded anything but glad. He sounded worried. Appalled. She must look a sight. By now the bruise had likely darkened.

Baron set the brake, got down from the wagon and came to Emily's side. After he helped her down, he introduced her properly to Henry and Elizabeth. Elizabeth ushered them inside to an elegant parlor where she had a tea service set out with some dainty cakes and cookies. The formal room with chandeliers and heavy drapes made her feel even more out of place.

"Sit down, dear," Elizabeth insisted. "I didn't know my brother was courting anyone in earnest, so this comes as a bit of a surprise. A lovely, lovely surprise."

Baron drew her to a brocaded chesterfield, gesturing for her to sit. Emily sat on the edge, feeling awkward and shabby amid such finery.

Emily accepted a cup of tea from Elizabeth. "He didn't court me."

Elizabeth stopped with a start. "I'm sorry, what?"

"Well…" Emily's words trailed off as she tried to think of what to say. She turned to Baron for help, but he just offered her a blank look. She took a sip of the tea, trying to buy some time. "I should say, we were acquainted. Wouldn't you say that, Mr. Calhoun?"

Both Henry and Elizabeth drew sharp breaths.

Baron set his hand on her arm. "Call me by my given name."

She took another sip of tea and said the word softly. "Baron."

Henry peered at her, studying her as if he wasn't sure what to think. "You never courted?"

"No." She gave Baron another bewildered look.

"I intended to offer for her today," Baron said. "I went to the mercantile to offer her uncle some incentive to give me his permission. Not that I need anyone's permission, but I didn't want Emily to suffer any slight. I wanted to avoid offending her uncle. When I arrived, I saw the bruises on her face."

Elizabeth winced. Emily averted her gaze, preferring to watch the tendril of steam rising from her tea. A scorching blaze of humiliation burned inside her. She couldn't stand to be looked at with pity.

Henry cleared his throat. "I assume you proposed properly to Emily."

"I didn't propose. I was trying to keep from murdering Roy Nelson. And get Emily to safety."

Henry shifted in his seat, turning his attention squarely on Baron. "I can't marry the two of you until you've proposed, and she's accepted."

Tension tightened Baron's features. "She's already accepted."

Neither man spoke for a moment.

"Accepted what?" Emily asked.

"Marriage. With me." Baron said.

"I don't have a proper dress. I only brought this simple muslin frock. I didn't bring any of my fancier dresses."

His eyes lit with understanding. "Good. I wouldn't allow you to wear them anyway."

Henry and Elizabeth looked at each other in bewilderment.

"Perhaps we should leave you alone," Elizabeth said stiffly, rising to her feet.

Henry nodded and got up from his chair. Elizabeth rose as well. Emily watched them with a rush of dismay. She took a sip of her tea, trying to tamp down her nervousness.

"You're leaving?" Emily asked. "Leaving me alone with Baron? Don't I need a chaperone?"

Baron scowled and followed them to the door. "You'll be fine, Emily. Henry will be nearby in case you scream for help. Won't you, Henry?"

Both Henry and Elizabeth ignored Baron's comments and left without a word. He closed the door behind him. Leaning against it, he folded his arms across his chest. The silence stretched between them for a long moment.

"I didn't always live like this," he said finally. "I have money because I worked for it. My first job was shoveling coal into a locomotive engine. I met a man on the train who worked as a bounty hunter. He told me how much he'd collected collaring criminals."

He pushed off the door, crossed the room and stood a few paces away. "It was a lot more than I made on the railroad, so, at eighteen, I started hunting outlaws."

She wasn't sure why he told her any of this but could easily picture him doing such rough work. He was a handsome, powerful man but one with an air of violence about him. She eyed his hands and wondered, with a barely suppressed shudder, if he'd ever raised them against a woman or child.

"I made more than other men because I went after the worst kind of criminals. After two years, I had enough money to buy land. I got a job in a bank, so I could learn about business. The years went by. Business was good. I suppose you could say I was blessed. Now, I have everything I want. Almost everything."

His eyes held her in a warm, entrancing gaze. She felt powerless to look away.

"You don't trust men. Your face is bruised. I understand your fear."

He drew closer, until he was so near she could have reached out to touch him. Lowering before her, he knelt upon one knee. He still was taller. She had to lift her gaze to meet his. She'd never been so close to him, or any man for that matter. His scent washed over her, making her thoughts spin. She looked into his eyes, noting the flecks of gold amidst the summer blue.

"I care for you, Emily. I'll always care for you. I can't make you marry me, but if you won't, I'll never marry."

His words stole her breath. *Never marry...*

She wanted to be his, but her long-held fears and shame left her tongue-tied.

"For me, there's only you. I offer you marriage, and if it's only a marriage of convenience, then I'm willing... more than willing."

"A marriage of convenience?" She stared at him in utter disbelief.

"I would like children, one day." His lips tilted. "I'm hoping you might grow to feel the same."

Too overwhelmed, she could only remain motionless before him. Her heart thundered in her chest. She could scarcely draw a breath.

He reached into his shirt pocket. Holding her in his gaze, he pulled out two tickets and offered them to her. They were two train tickets for first class passage to San Francisco.

Leaning closer, he took her hand in his, and whispered in her ear. "Will you marry me, Emily?"

He'd offered her more than she could have ever imagined, but even more than *what* he offered, was the tender, impassioned way he spoke to her. And the way he looked at her made her dare to believe in him, if only for a moment in time. Her throat felt tight and dry and she wasn't certain how she managed to give him an answer, but answer him she did.

She breathed the simple word. "Yes."

Chapter Twelve

Baron

Once Elizabeth and Henry were convinced that he didn't intend to drag Emily to the altar, they set about putting things in place. Elizabeth spoke with the servants and ordered a fine dinner. Henry, intent that Emily not spend a single night in Baron's home without being married, determined the ceremony should take place at sunset. He set off to find a suitable spot in the gardens.

Baron accompanied him but was little help. Mostly he was lost in his own thoughts. He followed Henry but let his gaze wander to the pastures stretching to the horizon. Horses grazed belly-deep in the hay fields.

The sight of the horses pleased him, but what had happened earlier in the parlor, pleased him even more. Emily had agreed. He'd seen the last shred of resistance crumble when he handed her the tickets. The train tickets had been a bit of a gamble, but the gesture had paid off. He'd intended to present her with the tickets at some point, but Henry and Elizabeth had undermined his plan with their meddlesome ways.

It didn't matter. Emily was happy. She was surprised and overcome. He'd never seen her look so sweet and unguarded as when she took the tickets from him. He'd be certain to surprise her with other gifts in the years to come. She didn't think he was a man of honor, probably because he'd practically kidnapped her, but over time, he'd prove his worth.

A shout from Henry drew his attention.

"It's perfect!" Henry stood between a pair of oaks, his arm outstretched. "The sun will set there. We can start the ceremony at six thirty. What do you think?"

Henry was not a man given to outbursts. He was quiet man, more given to long, ponderous silence, but his face was lit with a joyful smile. His eyes shone with delight at the picturesque location.

Baron nodded. "I think it will be fine."

The limbs swayed in the afternoon breeze. Leaves rustled. Henry was right. This was a perfect spot. Baron smiled as he pictured Emily standing beneath the enormous oaks. Elizabeth had offered her a dress. Even though he hadn't heard the details, he knew she'd be lovely.

Emily seemed to have no idea of how pretty she was. If anything, she tried to make herself look less attractive to avoid attention. It bothered him to think she'd *needed* to hide her beauty. His years as a bounty hunter, pursuing evil men, taught him more than he wanted to know about the darkness in men's hearts. Many women lived in fear of men. Many suffered untold cruelties. He was determined to shield Emily. He vowed to either make her forget her bad memories or give her new ones that would bring a smile to her lips.

With only an hour before sundown, Baron left Henry to his planning. He busied himself with shaving and dressing. The sun sank toward the horizon. Light slanted through the windows and Baron descended the stairs to find Henry and Elizabeth waiting in the entry.

"It's time," Elizabeth said, her eyes shone.

Baron went outside to wait at the appointed spot. Soon, Henry emerged from the house with Emily on his arm. Elizabeth trailed behind.

Emily stole his breath. She wore a light blue dress. Her hair hung down past her shoulders. Pale and wide-eyed, she held a small bouquet of tulips that shook in her trembling hands.

She handed the flowers to Elizabeth and set her hands in his. They felt cool, cold almost. When he wrapped his hands around hers, she shivered. The ceremony was short, thankfully. Henry pronounced them man and wife and Baron leaned down to brush a kiss across her lips. The instant before his lips pressed to hers, she turned her head. Instead of kissing her lips, his lips brushed her cheek.

She grew even more pale as she looked up at him, probably expecting some sort of rebuke. Instead, he lifted her hand to his lips. Surprise lit her eyes.

They retired to the house to enjoy dinner. It was just the four of them. Emily had no one to invite, not in Magnolia. He didn't either. His friends were more business associates than friends. He kept to himself, preferring things that way, and wondered if Emily would find life with him dull.

She sat to his right, talking with Henry and Elizabeth during dinner. She and Henry shared a conversation about books, particularly one they'd both just read about Lewis and Clark.

"You're quite well-read," Elizabeth marveled.

Emily blushed and stole a glance at Baron, giving him what seemed to be an apologetic look. "I like to read. I always have. I found a box of books in the mercantile. I didn't talk about it very much because my uncle and aunt might have taken them from me."

Elizabeth gave a small huff of displeasure.

Emily glanced at him once more.

"Did you bring them with you?" He arched his brow. "Or do I need to go back and get them?"

"I brought them with me."

"You and I are just alike, aren't we?"

"How so?" she asked.

"We both like books."

She pursed her lips, not believing him.

"And horses," he added.

Elizabeth sighed, smiling at them. "It was meant to be. A perfect match."

Baron watched Emily for her response, but she said nothing. Henry and Elizabeth chattered about perfect matches and such. Emily averted her gaze and gave a slight shake of her head.

Chapter Thirteen

Emily

After dinner, Emily and Baron bid Elizabeth and Henry goodnight. Baron ushered her upstairs to her room, his hand on her elbow. His fingers lent a gentle pressure. His grip was neither too forward, nor too tentative. He spoke amiably about how lovely she looked in her gown and that he hoped she found her room comfortable.

Throughout dinner and especially as they ascended the stairs, she'd expected him to say something about a wedding night or living together as man and wife. He said nothing about those subjects. Perhaps he'd been sincere when he'd offered a marriage of convenience.

"I'm not very talkative," he said. "Especially in the morning."

They walked down the hallway, approaching her room.

"That's fine," she said. "I won't trouble you." She eyed the door, her heart thundering in her chest.

"I won't be here every morning." He pushed open the door for her.

She stepped in, and he followed. Her panic edged up a notch, but subsided when he strolled around the room, restlessly checking the windows and peering out into the darkness.

"Where will you be, if not here?" she asked.

"I have to travel for business."

A small huff escaped her lips. She hadn't imagined that he'd leave her. She'd hardly had time to imagine he'd be her husband, truth be told, but the notion that he'd travel left her feeling bereft. Unmoored. A pit of despair grew heavily inside her heart. Maybe he had a woman that he kept for his visits. This was how some men lived, she reminded herself. A wife at home and a pretty little amusement in some other town.

"I want..." her words failed her.

He turned to face her, his eyes searching hers. He looked handsome as could be, dressed in his suit, his tie loosened, and his shirt unbuttoned at the neck.

"You want what, sweetheart?" A slow grin spread across his face. "Tell me and I'll get it. Just say the word."

"I want to go with you. If you travel, I should accompany you."

His smile faltered. And here he'd begin his fabrications, telling her it was no place for a woman. He needed her at home. She'd be a distraction or a burden.

He crossed the room, stopping abruptly a few paces from her. "You want to come? With me?"

"I do. It seems right for a wife to travel with her husband."

"All right. If you want to come, I'll take you." His expression softened. "I'd like that very much."

Her breath caught. She hadn't expected this response. Before she could reply, he went on.

"You'll need dresses and shoes and the like. I can't take my wife dressed in my sister's gowns, or in a muslin dress. Not that you don't look pretty as can be..." He smiled again and finished in a softer tone. "Always."

She shook her head. "You're very charming, aren't you? I'm sure you get your way with any woman you want. If not with your wealth, then with your fine words and silver tongue."

He loosened his tie, tugged it from his shirt collar and knit his brow as he considered her words. "Probably more with my wealth than my fine words. In fact, you're the first woman to tell me I was charming."

Not sure if she believed him or not, Emily stood silently watching him remove his cufflinks. A French door connected their rooms. She eyed it apprehensively, wondering how much he might undress in her room. After he finished with the cufflinks, he unbuttoned his coat. Thankfully, he stopped there.

"Most women," he continued, "say I'm rough-mannered, not charming."

She turned away, went to a chair and sank into the depths of the soft cushions, suddenly so very tired. Movement in a nearby mirror caught her attention. She studied her reflection, wincing at how dark the bruise had turned. She touched it with the tips of her fingers. The pain was a little less, even though it looked much worse.

"Rough-mannered is relative, isn't it?" she murmured.

He looked thoughtful. "Yes."

"Have you ever raised your hand-"

"Never."

An intensity burned in his eyes. She shivered. Despite the fire in his eyes, or maybe because of it, she believed him.

Chapter Fourteen

Baron

The final meeting of the day dragged on and on, trying his patience. He'd waited months for this day, a formal invitation to invest in the Presidio Cartel. Despite that, he wished it would end so he could go home to Emily. Instead, he sat with two men, one a member of the cartel, the other Baron's lawyer, Charles Stanton.

David Whittier, the youngest member of the cartel, explained how the Houston shipping channel had recently been dredged. The result was fifteen feet of depth. The deeper channel would allow larger ships to dock and larger ships meant greater revenue.

Baron eyed his lawyer. Charles probably wanted to talk about the churning, muddy waters of the shipping channel about as much as he wanted to swim from one bank to the other. No, Charles wanted the meeting to end, so he could discuss his daughter. He assumed Baron's investment in the cartel meant he intended to offer for Katherine. Baron still needed to explain that he'd taken a wife. He was sure Charles wouldn't receive the news well, but it couldn't be helped.

Baron didn't know the other man well. David Whittier came from a wealthy Texas family. Usually the sons of wealthy men had none of the drive their fathers had. They were more interested in parties and mistresses, sloth and gluttony. David seemed to be bright and ambitious too. He'd done some of the surveying of the channel himself, a fact that impressed Baron.

The meeting ground to a close. Finally. They made plans to meet formally at the Whittier Ranch to sign the agreement.

"That was some good work there, David," Baron offered as he shook the man's hand. "Next time, I'll come help survey the channel. Nothing I like better than learning the lay of the land. Especially if I'm about to invest in the land."

"Thank you, sir. I'll see myself out. I'm eager to start the trip home."

When the young man had left, Baron turned to Charles. "I have some good news."

Charles blinked several times in confusion. "News...?"

"I've married."

The blood drained from Charles's face. He moved away, slowly walking to a chair near the window. "I see. That comes as a bit of a surprise."

"It was a surprise to me too. It all happened very quickly."

Charles took out a handkerchief and wiped his brow. "Quickly?"

Baron frowned. "I didn't marry because I had to marry, if that's what you're thinking. I married because I realized I'd been in love with the girl for some time. She was in some danger, and I wanted to remove her from the threat."

Charles nodded and sighed heavily. "I'll admit that I don't relish the idea of telling Katherine."

Baron gritted his teeth. There were several other men who would say the same, as if he owed them something. He might have dined in their homes once or twice and paid the wife and daughter a compliment over the food or furnishings or anything really. With just a few words of praise, the fathers often had Baron as good as married.

For the sake of their friendship, Baron didn't disclose any of his thoughts.

Charles rubbed his temple and let his hand fall to his lap. "What do you think of David Whittier?"

Baron found the question odd but didn't say as much. "Seems fine. He's a hard worker."

"He's a single man."

"As far as I know."

"Maybe I'll send him an invitation to dinner."

Baron chuckled as he wandered closer to the window. "You didn't take long to find my replacement."

"I'm motivated. Katherine and her mother bicker every minute of the day. If I can marry my daughter off, I might be able to enjoy a little peace and quiet in the evenings."

Charles gathered his things, grumbling about quarrelsome wives and daughters. Baron felt sorry for him but felt grateful too. While he'd been married for only a few days, he wed a woman who made him yearn to go home in the evenings. He was certain that one day he and Emily would have a close bond as husband and wife. It would take time, but that mattered little to him.

Later that evening, when he walked through his front door, he was greeted by the savory aroma of dinner. Elizabeth's voice drifted down the hallway. Emily spoke too, her voice coming from the direction of the sitting room. He walked briskly, eager to see his bride.

Emily sat with her back to the door, sketching a picture of Elizabeth. His sister sat on the chesterfield across the room. Henry relaxed near the window, reading a novel in the fading rays of dusk.

The floorboards creaked beneath his weight. Emily turned in her chair and gave him a small smile. He wanted to reach for her, to wrap her in his arms.

Emily touched her lips with the tip of her finger to silence him. For a moment, he couldn't understand her meaning, but then he saw what she had on her lap. She sketched Elizabeth's face. His sister looked thoughtful, youthful and pretty. The sight made Baron smile. He could imagine how much his sister would like the picture. Elizabeth wasn't a particularly vain woman, but any woman would be pleased to see a pretty picture of herself.

"That's lovely," he murmured.

"I want to surprise her," Emily said under her breath.

"I won't say a word."

"Baron," his sister exclaimed. "There you are, sneaking in like a thief in the night. Henry and I were just discussing how you should take Emily on a honeymoon. Spoil her a little. Isn't that right, Henry?"

"Yes, dear." Henry started, looked up and smiled at Baron as if just then noticing him. "Ah, Baron. So nice to see you."

"Henry. Did you find a good book?"

He held the book up. "Rereading Tom Sawyer. It's a fine piece of writing."

Elizabeth got to her feet and ushered them out of the sitting room and down to the dining room to eat dinner. They passed the evening in amiable conversation, with Emily playing the part of his wife. Just before they retired for the evening, Emily offered Elizabeth the sketch she'd drawn.

While Baron enjoyed his sister's delight, he kept his gaze fixed upon Emily. As Elizabeth went on about the picture and how she'd always cherish it, Emily blushed. She bit her lip, glanced shyly at him and quickly averted her eyes. He'd never seen her look so nervous. Warmth flooded his chest. He wanted to go to her and fold her in his arms.

Henry rose from his chair and stood behind Elizabeth's chair. He marveled at Emily's skill, hardly able to tear his gaze from the picture. His praise only made Emily's blush deepen.

"I've always thought my wife is beautiful," he said. "I fell in love with her the moment I first met her."

"Oh, Henry, hush." Elizabeth fussed. "You didn't either. You were eating an ice cream cone, flicking flies away."

Henry nodded. "It's true, but then I saw Elizabeth, a vision in a beautiful, pale pink dress."

Elizabeth smiled. "It was pink, wasn't it?"

"And I promptly dropped my cone." Henry said solemnly. "I felt as though I'd been thunderstruck. Thankfully, Elizabeth stopped to offer her sympathy over the ice cream."

Elizabeth smiled, but didn't say more.

Henry pointed to the drawing. "Somewhere along the way, throughout the years, one stops noticing the little things they love so well."

Elizabeth frowned. "One does?"

"Yes," Henry said. "You don't really see as well any more. The familiarity breeds a sort of blindness, I suppose."

"Henry, what on earth are you talking about?" Elizabeth gave him a stern look. "Blindness? Familiarity?"

"That's right. I remember the first time we spoke. You told me what a shame it was that I'd dropped the ice cream, but the way you said it, with a small smile playing on your lips, is just how Emily has captured you in the drawing. It's quite astonishing."

Elizabeth returned her attention to the picture. "I didn't know I smiled in that way."

Henry bent down to kiss the top of his wife's head. "You do. And it's lovely. I would like very much to have that picture, Emily. I want to frame it and put it in my study."

Elizabeth feigned indignation but gave him the picture. As she rose from the chair, Baron noted her smile and saw what Henry meant. He found himself smiling too. The only person who wasn't smiling was Emily, who looked distressed.

"It's not very good," she said. "I don't think you should frame it."

Henry grumbled, walked out of the dining room and muttered a few words about the picture being the loveliest piece of art he owned. Elizabeth gave a girlish laugh as she followed him out and told Henry he was nothing more than a flatterer.

Baron went to Emily, tucked her hand in his and tried to comfort her. "It is a beautiful drawing. I think you've made both Henry and Elizabeth very happy. Thank you."

She smiled gratefully at him. His heart warmed as he fought the urge to brush a kiss across her lips. At times, simply being near her filled him with happiness. He reminded himself that being close to her was all he could hope for, at least for now.

It was only later, when he lay in bed alone, that he felt the pangs of loneliness.

Before Emily, he'd never suffered a moment of loneliness. He'd been glad to be alone. He cared for Elizabeth and Henry, of course, but aside from them, he enjoyed keeping to himself. Now, he lay in bed, listening for sounds of Emily in the next room. He'd deliberately left the door ajar for that reason. He heard the sheets rustling. A soft sigh. Then nothing more.

He tried to suppress a growl of frustration. He'd promised her a marriage of convenience and felt a pang of guilt for wishing for something more. The reason he wished for more was because he suspected she wished for more. There were little moments here and there, when he saw sweet yearning in her eyes, and despite his conscience, he began to think of ways he might coax her to be more at ease with him. Maybe a trip would be just the thing. She wanted to travel with him? He'd oblige her.

He'd plan a special trip, a trip to court and woo his nervous bride.

Chapter Fifteen

Emily

Baron offered to take her to Fort Worth to shop for dresses and the like.

Emily wasn't sure if she was flattered or worried. Perhaps a little of both. She persuaded Baron to wait a week until her bruise faded. Elizabeth and Henry promised to keep things running smoothly on the ranch. Elizabeth took Emily's measurements and mailed them to her best tailor, so they could begin work.

After Emily and Baron arrived in Fort Worth, they checked into the Regency Hotel. The rooms were magnificent. Emily wandered the halls, her steps echoing on the marble. Paintings adorned the walls, oil portraits of notable Fort Worth citizens. Several rooms had balconies that overlooked a park with fountains. She would have liked to explore more of the apartment, but Baron whisked her out the door.

"Let's see what the dress shops have for you," he said, offering his arm.

"All right." She took his arm, feeling a sense of dread creep over her.

They descended the wide stairs and crossed the grand salon of the hotel, beneath the glittering chandeliers and past the porters and bellman. Men dressed in fine suits strolled past talking amongst themselves, some were accompanied by ladies clad in elegant gowns. The women wore fine jewels, dazzling gems, or gleaming pearls.

The jewels, the pearls especially, reminded her of the gifts her mother received from her admirers. Her mother always tried to hide her gentleman callers, but Emily would sneak away from her nurses and hide behind a potted palm in the hallway to eavesdrop. She'd listen to the way the men heaped praise on her mother's fine eyes or lovely tresses. Their flattery always made her stomach turn.

Emily had especially disliked one man in particular. The man had made her mother cry.

Each time he came, he brought jewelry for her mother, always pearls. Emily would steal into her mother's room, take the jewels and hide them. Somehow her mother found out. Always. She'd search Emily's room, finding the pearls easily. Her mother just shook her head, never reprimanding her.

As Emily walked with Baron, she could almost picture her mother, dangling the pearls, gazing at them with dismay.

If Reginald were truly sorry, he'd bring me gems, not pearls.

Her mother's eyes were red-rimmed as they always were when Reginald visited, but the sorrow never kept her from wearing the pearls.

Of all her mother's friends, Emily had disliked Reginald the most because he always made her mother so sad. Her mother liked to tell her that men were meant to be managed, but she forgot her advice the moment he came to visit. When he left, she often took to her bed for days, leaving Emily alone with her nursemaid.

Baron had given her a gold band when they exchanged vows. She eyed it as they walked, somehow pleased he hadn't given her something lavish.

"Let me spoil you," Baron said gently. "Would you?"

Her stomach clenched. Gifts and trinkets would lead to expectations and demands and ultimately betrayal. She wanted to trust him. She sensed the first glimmers of trust and that frightened her almost more than anything she'd ever known. "You don't need to buy me pretty things."

"I want to buy you everything your heart desires."

He stopped amidst the bustling crowd. "Your wish is my command."

"You're very kind," she said, half-believing her own words.

Frowning, he ushered her out of the hotel. "I'm not being kind, or at least not in the general sense. I want to make you happy. Be kind to *you*. What do you like? Gold? Gems? Pearls?"

She drew a sharp breath. They walked a short way before she spoke. "Did you know," she murmured, "pearls dissolve in vinegar?"

"I did not." Arching his brow, he invited her to elaborate.

"It's true."

"You read about this in a book?"

"Yes." She answered tentatively and then added, "But I've tried it myself."

"I'm sure there's more to that story." His lips curved into a smile as he ushered her into a dressmaker's shop. Peabody's Fine Ladies Apparel.

Peabody's wasn't the first fancy dress shop Emily had ever stepped into. She'd had plenty of fine dresses made before in New Orleans, but it was the first time she'd been escorted by a gentleman, and this man was her husband. The notion shocked her to her core each time she considered it. The shopkeepers made at least as big a fuss over Baron as they did her. They offered him a refreshment and sandwiches and cakes. He dismissed their offers, thanking them for the trouble.

A shopkeeper led her to the back where she was to change into her new gown. A dress hung on a brass hook. A sumptuous deep azure gown made of gauzy silk. She ran her fingertips over the sleeve. Her heart thrilled at wearing something other than the dress Elizabeth had lent her, or the muslin dress she'd worn for so long. The blue would suit her eyes, or so she liked to think.

Would Baron like it?

She turned the question over in her mind.

The shopkeeper helped her into the dress and tied the ribbons at the back. It was beautiful. The gown made her feel pretty and feminine and she loved it more than she'd imagined.

"Shall we show Mr. Calhoun?" The woman asked. "I'm sure he'll approve. You look lovely."

Emily felt a wave of awkwardness and didn't reply immediately.

Outside the dressing room, Baron chuckled. "Come, sweetheart. I'll see the dress soon enough."

She went outside and stood before him, her discomfort growing.

He smiled. "You look beautiful."

She blushed. "You hardly looked at the dress."

"You always look beautiful."

"Do you want me to get it?"

He shrugged. "I want what you want, Emily."

His words surprised her. His tone and the look in his eye stole her breath. Beside her, the shopkeeper set her hand on her heart and sighed.

"How romantic," she said. "Young love always takes my breath away."

If Baron noticed the woman's reaction, he gave no sign. "I do, in fact, want what you want. That's all I've ever wanted. And to have you by my side. That too."

"That's so sweet," the woman murmured.

Emily turned to the woman. "I'll take the dress."

"She'll need a dozen, just to start," Baron said.

Emily laughed and shook her head. "I thought you said you want what I want."

"I do want what you want." He smiled. "Just more of it."

Chapter Sixteen

Baron

Baron intended to spend three days in Fort Worth with Emily. He wanted to take her shopping during the day and to the finest restaurants each evening. On the day they were to head back to Magnolia, he received word that a building in downtown Fort Worth was for sale. The owner was eager to sell the four-story structure, and an eager seller always meant a bargain.

He waited for Emily to join him for breakfast on the hotel room's veranda. The servant set out coffee, a bowl of citrus fruit and various breakfast dishes. Baron's stomach rumbled. A moment after the hotel servant left, Emily appeared dressed in a gown the color of a winter sunset. Not quite orange, but not quite red. If he were a more cultured man, he might know the exact name.

The dress maker had made many beautiful dresses for his wife. He could hardly tear his eyes from her, but when she blushed, he looked away, not wanting to make her uncomfortable. He rose and held out the chair for her. A lovely fragrance wafted from her milky skin, making him want to draw closer, but he refrained.

"There's been a change of plans," he said, filling her coffee cup. "Instead of returning to Magnolia today, we'll remain in Fort Worth a little longer. Maybe two days."

She nodded and poured cream into her coffee. "All right."

"I have an appointment at eleven. I'm going to look at a building that's for sale. It shouldn't take more than two or three hours."

"You're going without me?"

"I thought you might like some time to yourself."

Instead of responding, she lowered her gaze. She added a sugar cube to her coffee, some cream, and lifted the cup to her lips. Every gesture suggested that she was hurt. He watched, not understanding. Her hands curled around the edge of the China as if she wanted to warm her hands. The air was cool. A light breeze carried a slight chill.

"Are you cold?" he asked.

"A little," she said quietly. "I get cold easily. I should get my wrap."

"I'll get it for you." Before she could protest, he got to his feet and went inside. Her wrap, a drab woolen swath, lay over the back of a chair. He studied it as he walked back to the table. The frayed edges suggested it was well-loved. One day, he'd get her something finer. Stepping behind her, he draped it over her narrow shoulders.

She shivered. When she gathered it around herself, he imagined holding her in his arms and chasing the chill from her as he folded her into his embrace. He yearned to touch her but didn't dare. Not yet.

"I'd like to accompany you," she said.

"And I would enjoy your company."

Her eyes widened. She blinked. "You would?"

"Of course, I would. I didn't want to ask."

"Why not?"

"I think it might bore you. Just a few men wandering around a dusty, empty building."

She sipped her coffee and served herself some of the fruit.

He leaned back in his chair and observed the flare of dismay behind her eyes. She fretted. Yet she held her tongue, not wanting to reveal her thoughts to him.

"You don't believe me?" he asked quietly.

She gave a small, feminine shrug. "Seeing is believing."

"Then come."

She tested him. Why? Did she doubt that he wanted to be with her every moment of the day?

An hour later, they arrived at the steps of the building and Baron helped her down from the buggy. The land agent, Pierre Savoy, stood at the top of the steps with his assistant. They waited between massive stone columns. Both men stared at Emily with more interest than Baron liked. While he was proud of squiring Emily around town, he didn't care for the way some men eyed his lovely wife.

"Mr. Savoy," Baron said. "Thank you for meeting with us this morning."

Savoy didn't take his gaze from Emily. Baron introduced her to him. Baron could see that Savoy would have liked to take Emily's hand, but she avoided his touch, hanging back and clinging to his arm with both of her hands.

"It's very nice to meet you," she said softly.

"The pleasure is entirely mine," Savoy said, with a heavy French accent.

Emily remained quiet for most of the morning, staying close to his side. They walked the empty halls, their footsteps echoing across the marble. Mr. Savoy told them of the building's history. The owner had just decided to part with the building, and while it hadn't been available for long, it would likely sell quickly.

Baron doubted that. Mr. Savoy's account was a different story than the account Baron had heard. The note he'd received that morning from Charles Stanton was that the owner needed to sell. Quickly.

Pierre Savoy droned on about the building. He spoke of the fine materials. The excellent location. Fort Worth's booming cattle trade.

Beyond the teller windows lay the office of the bank manager. A vault sat, its door open, its shelves empty. With a playful smile, Baron led her into the safe's chamber. While he had to duck his head as he walked through the doorway, the room itself allowed him to stand straight.

Emily's looked around with a small smile on her lips. "I've never been inside a safe."

"Neither have I."

An ebony tendril had escaped her chignon. He wanted to grasp it between his fingers and find out if it was as soft as it looked. What would it feel like to trail his fingers through the thick mass? He pushed those thoughts away.

He patted her hand. "We won't be much longer."

"I'm not bored. I'm glad to have a moment with you."

His gaze dropped to the curve of her mouth. She'd denied him a kiss when they married and he had the urge to pull her close and claim her sweet kiss, right here in the musty safe.

"You're glad?" he asked.

Her lips quirked. "I overheard Mr. Savoy when he spoke with his assistant earlier."

Baron hadn't understood their conversation because the two men spoke in French.

"The owner would like ten thousand for the building. However, he's come upon difficult times and would take six," she said softly.

He grinned and lowered to whisper in her ear. "You realize you're going to have to travel with me all the time. Everywhere. I'll insist."

"You might grow tired of me."

"Never."

She looked at him with a look in her eye that made him think she didn't believe him. The expression, a flicker of vulnerability, made him wish for the thousandth time he could find a way to show her he was devoted to her. She couldn't know that she owned his heart. He would need to spend the rest of his days showing her how much he loved her.

He prided himself on his powers of persuasion. The problem? The more he tried to get close to Emily, the more she retreated. Her reticence exasperated him, but even more, it left a dull ache in his chest. It pained him to think of Emily enduring any pain or danger in her past. He hated the pain he saw in her eyes whenever she allowed herself to have an unguarded moment.

What had happened to his sweet wife that made her so afraid to trust him?

Chapter Seventeen

Emily

Marriage to Baron Calhoun meant plans could change from one day to the next. He'd told her that once he'd completed the purchase of the bank building, they would return to Magnolia. Over breakfast the next morning, he informed her they would be traveling to Houston instead.

She didn't mind. In fact, it pleased her that he wanted her to accompany him on his travels. Despite that, she couldn't help teasing him a little over breakfast.

"What about my trip to San Francisco? I'm not going to see an ocean sunset in Houston."

They sat on the terrace, the morning sunshine warming the lovely spot. The hotel overlooked a park. In the distance, children's laughter mixed with the twitter of birds. The fragrance of roses wafted on the edge of a soft breeze. Baron sat across from her, dressed in a suit and tie, looking dapper despite, or perhaps because of, his wind-ruffled hair.

"And I'm anxious to take you. The meeting in Houston is very important to me. I'm considering joining a group that has shipping and mining interests throughout Texas."

The skin on the back of her neck prickled. Her mother's gentleman callers all seemed to know each other and many owned companies that held mining and shipping interests. She shook off the discomfort, but not before Baron noticed.

"I'm a man of my word, Emily. I promised to take you to California, and I intend to."

"I know. I can see that you're a..." Her words faded as she searched for the word that would adequately describe her husband.

He arched his brow, reached for a biscuit from the basket and waited for her to finish. Her face warmed. She sipped her tea to buy herself a little time. He buttered the biscuit and added a dollop of jelly. Amusement sparked in his eyes. Clearly, he enjoyed her discomfort.

"You have, thus far, treated me very well," she managed.

"Thus far? It sounds as if you're reserving judgment."

"I am a cautious person."

He chuckled. "You are that. I intend to treat you well for the rest of my days. I also intend to convince you that you owe me something."

"Convince me?"

She let her gaze drift from his eyes to his broad chest and to his hands. Baron might do business with other powerful men, but at his heart he was a man who preferred his ranch and horses. He wasn't born to a life of luxury. He was a man who required hard work to exhaust his formidable energy.

As she eyed his hands, she wondered what he meant by convincing her. And she wondered what she owed him.

His smile faded. "Don't look so afraid, Emily. I'm not a monster. I wouldn't ever want to frighten you. I am, however, not above tormenting you to get what I want." He took a bite of the biscuit.

Emily blinked. "I don't know what you mean. I must say no one has ever told me something so... so, outrageous. Torment me? For what? What do you want?"

"To kiss my wife."

106

"A kiss?"

"Yes. You didn't allow me to kiss you when we said our vows. I'm not even sure our marriage is valid without a kiss."

"Not *valid*?"

He took a swallow of coffee. "We'll travel to San Francisco in a few weeks, and if you haven't succumbed to my charms, I intend to toss you over my shoulder, march down to the water's edge and throw you into the icy waves of the Pacific."

He chuckled. The look of amusement returned, lighting his eyes with a wicked gleam. He leaned back in his chair, a smug smile curving his mouth. He was the picture of arrogance.

"You *could* save yourself," he said. "All you need to do is kiss me. Once. Otherwise it's into the ocean for you. They say the water is quite cold. Might be uncomfortable. I know how cold-natured you are."

"You wouldn't." She shook her head and pursed her lips to keep from smiling along with him. The idea was so absurd it was beneath much of a response. He wanted to bait her. He wanted a shocked and horrified reaction from her. She refused to give him the satisfaction.

"Do you know how to swim?" he asked, feigning concern.

"I refuse to discuss this with you. You're being..." Again, she found herself searching for words.

"Decisive?"

"Please." She waved a dismissive hand. "Childish."

He grinned. "I offered a marriage in name only, but the bride still needs to kiss the groom. It's understood. I'm insisting on a kiss for *your* sake, not mine. I want you to rest easy, knowing that our vows are complete."

She shook her head. He could tease her as much as he wanted. Nothing would convince her to kiss him. That would never happen. She'd never allow herself to kiss him for the simple reason that kissing Baron would overwhelm her beyond anything she could ever imagine.

While she enjoyed their banter, it simply deepened her resolve never to allow herself a single moment of weakness. Baron was sly and might be willing to try underhanded tactics to get her to kiss him. It was impossible. A kiss would be the beginning of the end. Despite her misgivings, her lips tingled as she imagined what it would feel like to kiss him.

He gazed at her, a thoughtful expression on his features. "I always thought women liked to be kissed. Not you?"

"How would I know?" The words tumbled from her lips before she could properly consider her reply. She'd revealed far more than she intended.

"Emily," he said quietly. "You've never been kissed?"

The playfulness was gone from his voice. She cringed, wishing they were discussing anything other than if she'd ever been kissed. How had the conversation taken such a precarious turn? She searched his eyes, half-expecting to see pity. Pity would have been easier to tolerate than the tenderness she saw in their depths. He held her in his gaze, waiting.

"I haven't ever been kissed, if you must know."

He nodded. Silence stretched between them for a long moment. Finally, he broke the silence. "You don't have to kiss me, if you're so set against kissing."

She expected him to say more, to tell her he was only teasing about tossing her in the ocean. But he said nothing more about his absurd threat. When he gave her the train tickets, she'd tucked them away. Over the last few weeks, the prospect of traveling with Baron to the Pacific Ocean had taken shape in her mind. She imagined walking the beach with him and watching the sun descend into the distant horizon.

I'm a man of my word...

His words echoed in her mind. She knew this to be true, but surely, he teased her when he threatened to carry her out into the ocean and drop her into the icy waves. She tried to reassure herself that his threat was just a playful bit of banter. Baron would never subject her to such treatment just because she'd evaded his kiss.

She was certain. Mostly certain.

Chapter Eighteen

Baron

The next night, they left Houston aboard an evening train that would take them to San Antonio. Their car offered two bedrooms, a shared washroom and a small sitting room. He glimpsed Emily moving around her room, setting her things away. Once she'd caught him spying on her and gave him a cheeky smile. He expected her to close the door, but she left it open.

In the past, he'd always traveled alone. Throughout the years, he'd had various assistants but never found one that suited him. Certainly, never one that he imagined traveling with.

"I like being near you," he said as he adjusted his cufflinks.

He grimaced at his clumsy words. They were true. If anything, they were an understatement. It wasn't so much that he liked being near her but found the idea of being parted from her unbearable.

"I like being near you," she replied lightly.

He let out a sigh of contentment. Yesterday morning he'd spoken rashly, threatening to toss his bride into the ocean. He couldn't imagine what had come over him. Since then, she'd regarded him with a slight wariness, but there were a few times where he'd caught her gazing at his lips. When she realized he noticed her attention, she blushed a lovely pink.

She worried about his threat. If he were a gentleman, he'd assure her that he'd been only teasing. And yet, it pleased him that she *might* be imagining a kiss between them. His conscience troubled him, but not enough to take back his words. All's fair in love and war, he told himself.

"I have a surprise for you." He went to the doorway and nudged the door open.

Trunks filled the room. Dresses spilled out of the top. Her drawing pad and pencils sat on a table by the window. He let his gaze drift across the room, greedily drinking in the feminine details. Ribbons, hair brushes, silken gowns. The edge of a petticoat peeked from a trunk in the corner.

"A surprise?" she asked, her tone edged with suspicion. "Should I be worried?"

"I don't think so." He reached into his coat pocket. "I meant what I said. I do like being near you, not just because I enjoy your company, but because you have a sharp, quick mind."

She turned from her unpacking and looked at him with surprise.

"You are smart, Emily. Surely, I'm not the first person to tell you that." He held a bank book in his hands. Stepping into her room, he picked his way through the disarray and handed her the small bank register.

She took it from him and slowly opened it. Her lips parted. She drew a sharp breath.

"A bank account, in my name?"

He nodded. "Yes. I didn't want to take you to see the building in Fort Worth. Most women would have found that kind of thing to be dull. Not only did you go, but you saved me four thousand dollars."

Her eyes widened. "You're giving me four thousand dollars?"

"I am."

She glanced down at the book. "Your name isn't on this account."

"Because it's not my money. It's yours."

"I see," she whispered. "It's mine."

"I'm going to take you with me to help me with all my transactions."

He put his hands in his pockets and smiled at the sweet expression on her face. Wonder filled her eyes. A small huff of disbelief fell from her lips.

"It's too much, Baron." She gestured to the gowns and shoes and trunks that filled the room. "You've already spoiled me."

Her voice trembled. He'd hoped she would be pleased with the bank account in her name, but he wondered if he'd inadvertently stirred up unhappy memories. He gritted his teeth, fighting the urge to wrap her in his arms and soothe her fears.

"I haven't begun to spoil you, Emily."

There was a knock at the door in his room.

"That must be our dinner." He excused himself, went to his room and admitted the porter. The man wheeled in a cart with a silver dinner service. The aroma of roast beef wafted through the air. Baron gave him a tip and saw him out. When he turned, he found Emily standing by the table, gazing at the spread of food.

"I keep thinking that I'm dreaming," she said. "A wonderful dream that's all going to come to a crashing end."

He came to her side.

"When I was a girl, my mother sent me to the finest schools and took me on lovely trips. And then one day it was all over.

Not only had she died, but I discovered everything about my life was a lie."

The pain in her voice made his heart ache. He held his hands out, palms up. "There's no lie here. I'm concealing nothing from you. And one day, you can tell me about your life, about your mother, anything."

She bit her lip. Her eyes watered, and she turned away. "My past is painful to me."

"Then we won't talk about it." He pulled a chair from the table and gestured for her to sit. "Instead, we'll talk about the future."

Chapter Nineteen

Emily

They arrived in San Antonio late morning and went directly to the hotel. Once inside their room, a bellman delivered a telegram from Henry and Elizabeth. They intended to come to San Antonio to visit them the next day. Baron arranged for them to stay in a suite down the hall.

Baron spent much of the day looking over business proposals to prepare for the meeting with the Presidio Cartel that was to take place in several days' time.

Emily sat on the balcony overlooking the town square. On the corner, a shoe-shine boy worked busily. She sketched him as he toiled.

"I meant to squire you around town," Baron said as he came to the door. "Instead, I had to read a pile of reports. I wish I'd spent the day with you. I'm sorry."

"I don't mind. I kept myself busy." She turned her sketch pad to show him her drawing.

He took the pad from her and studied her sketch. A twinge of awkwardness crept over her. She was unaccustomed to showing her work to others and still wasn't used to Baron's praise. He encouraged her in everything. His admiration was genuine, not simple flattery.

"When I look at your sketch, I can almost smell the boot polish," he said.

She laughed softly.

"I'd like to take you to dinner. Tonight, I'll have you all to myself. Tomorrow, I'll have to share you with Henry and Elizabeth." He handed the pad back to her. "I'm sure that my sister has come to make sure I'm treating you well."

"I have no complaints." She smiled as she got to her feet and pulled her shawl close, to guard against the late afternoon chill.

He leaned against the doorway, filling it with his broad shoulders. His gaze drifted from her eyes, lower to her lips and slowly back to her eyes. The quirk of his mouth sent her thoughts to the beach in California, him allowing her to walk in front, then being picked up, thrown over his shoulder and carried toward the icy cold ocean. Did he really intend to carry out that ridiculous threat? She shivered.

"Are you cold, sweetheart?" His tone held a slight teasing edge.

"A little, perhaps."

He blocked the doorway and seemed to be in no hurry to get out of her way. When he crossed his arms over his chest, she was certain he toyed with her. Fortunately, she had a tactic to disarm him.

"I can't wait to see Elizabeth tomorrow." She tried to keep from smiling at his look of annoyance. "It will be nice to have time to visit with her."

He frowned.

"May I step past you, Mr. Calhoun?"

His gaze dropped to her lips again. "I haven't decided."

With her index finger, she poked his side, drawing a surprised yelp from him. He swatted her hand away. She was too fast, however, and managed another jab.

"Ticklish, Mr. Calhoun?"

"Emily, stop. I'm warning you."

He tried to fend off any more jabs and relented, stepping back to allow Emily a chance to dart past him. She snickered as she hurried to her room.

"I'm getting ready for dinner."

He didn't reply or pursue her and his lack of a response disappointed her. She'd enjoyed teasing him. The man deserved a small taste of his own medicine.

When she emerged from her room, clad in an evening frock, she found him in the sitting room reading. He glanced up and gazed at her with a soft look in his eyes. Every so often he'd give her a look filled with such tenderness that it stole her breath.

Outside the hotel, he offered his arm and they strolled through the streets. They dined at a restaurant that overlooked a river. After dinner, he hailed a carriage and asked the driver to show them the town's sights.

Baron was gallant and charming. When he noticed she was chilled, he wrapped his jacket around her shoulders. When he saw she grew tired, he had the driver take them back to the hotel.

"I'll have to drop you at the back entrance, sir. Only hotel carriages are allowed at the front door."

"Absolutely not," Baron countered. "I won't have my wife walk along an alley this time of the night."

"I'm sorry, sir. It's either that or drop you a block over from the hotel. If I don't follow the rules, they'll make trouble for me."

"A block from the hotel is better than a dark, back alley."

The carriage stopped a short distance from the hotel. Baron helped Emily down and paid the driver. His dark expression made her shiver, and the sound of his voice, a deeper timbre than usual, filled her with unease. Their footsteps echoed in the quiet streets.

Tugging her closer, Baron wrapped a protective arm around her shoulders. Never before had he held her so near. A thrill of pleasure warmed her. Normally, she avoided his touch. Now, she wondered why she'd been so foolish. There was no harm in nestling close to her husband who only wanted to keep her safe.

"Why are we walking so quickly?" she asked.

"I'll tell you inside. The carriage dropped us off further than he promised."

Before she could say another word, Baron stopped. Following his gaze, Emily saw two men standing in the shadows. They blocked the street, preventing Emily and Baron from advancing.

"What do we have here?" one of them rasped.

The men advanced, walking slowly. Emily stood rooted to the spot, too terrified to speak or move. In the shadows, she saw the glint of a knife. Baron must have seen it too, for in the next instant, he sprang into action. The men yelled in surprise.

Baron grabbed them and brought their heads together with a sickening crack. They howled with pain. The knife clattered to the street. The men fled into the night. It was over in an instant. Emily hadn't had time to cry out.

Baron emerged from the shadows, his mouth a grim line. Without a word, he took her hand and ushered her to the hotel entrance. A doorman stood outside. He greeted them, wishing them a pleasant evening.

"I trust you had..." the doorman's words faded. "Sir! Your arm. You're bleeding."

Emily looked at Baron's arm and blanched. The sleeve was drenched in blood.

"It's just a small cut," Baron growled.

"You're hurt," Emily whispered. "You're bleeding."

"It's fine."

They stood in the entrance. A crowd gathered. Their voices seemed distant, their words indistinct. The world tilted. She swayed and lifted her hand to her mouth, a response to the queasiness.

The edges of her vision darkened. Everything seemed to swim around her as she fell forward. He caught her, lifted her in his arms. Her world went silent.

Chapter Twenty

Baron

The hotel physician frowned at Baron, looking affronted. The man wanted to examine Emily and took offense that Baron insisted on remaining in the room during the examination. Baron held a swath of gauze to his forearm to stanch the flow of blood from his wound.

"I assume you're an adequate doctor... of decent moral fiber, but I won't allow you to go near my wife. Not when she's unconscious."

The man sputtered, clutched his medical bag and grew more red-faced by the minute.

"Your suggestion that I shouldn't examine my patient without another person present implies that I have some sordid intention."

Baron tossed the blood-soaked gauze in the rubbish basket but then thought better of it. If Emily saw blood, she might faint again. He picked the fabric out of the trash. He tucked it in an empty box he spied in the corner of his wardrobe.

"I'm not debating your intentions, doc." Baron felt him slip back into his more informal speech, the way he'd spoken when he was a bounty hunter. Primitive, protective instincts sprang to life. "I'm sure they're as pure as the driven snow. You're still not stepping foot in that room without me."

"Bah – fine. Let's get this over with. I still need to tend to your arm."

Baron followed him into the bedroom, his gaze going to where Emily lay on her bed. A lamp flickered on a corner table. Emily rested, curled on her side, a blanket covering her to protect her from the evening chill. When he brought her to their room, he lay her down on her bed, tucked a blanket around her and sat nearby.

She hadn't stirred at all.

"Mrs. Calhoun," the doctor said gently as he set his hand on her shoulder. "Can you hear me?"

Emily's lids fluttered. She sighed and frowned at the doctor. "Where's Baron?"

Baron smiled. She'd asked for him. It felt like some sort of victory. He was doubly glad that he'd insisted on being in the room when the doctor examined her.

"I'm here, sweetheart," he replied, coming to the foot of the bed.

Her gaze drifted down his arm and rested on his wound. She closed her eyes. A soft moan escaped her lips as she shuddered. Baron had never seen her so pale and frightened and the sight of her in such a state of distress affected him deeply.

"Try not to upset yourself," the doctor said. "I'm going to give you something for your nerves. Tell me, Mrs. Calhoun, are you with child?"

Emily lay with her eyes closed. His question drew a surprised response from her. Her eyes flew open. "I am not. Nor will I ever be."

The doctor gave Baron an inquisitive look. Baron ignored him.

"All right, my dear," the doctor said with a weary sigh. "I'll give you medicine to calm your mind. You'll sleep very well and might not remember anything, but you'll waken refreshed."

He poured a small vial of powder into a glass of water and offered it to Emily. She drank it, made a face and fell back to the pillow. An instant later, she dozed, snoring softly.

The next half hour, Baron endured the doctor's ministrations. The man insisted on stitching the wound on Baron's arm. It didn't hurt, not near as much as other injuries he'd suffered over the years. He'd much prefer to send the physician away, but he didn't, for the simple reason that Emily would be distressed to see his wound. He needed it stitched and bandaged.

Finally, the doctor finished tending to Baron's wounds.

"Your wife will sleep soundly till noon," he said before departing. "Just to be safe, you should remain close to her throughout the night."

"I beg your pardon?" Baron snapped, his patience waning.

The man shrugged. "Sometimes women sleepwalk after taking the draught. Nothing to worry about. Not with a young, attentive husband sleeping next to her. Just keep one eye open and you'll do fine."

The doctor turned and shuffled out the door.

Baron grimaced and shut the door, bolting the locks and securing the chain. Would Emily sleepwalk? He growled softly, returning to her bedroom. Gently, he nudged the door open. She wasn't in the bed. He shoved the door aside and stormed into the bedroom. She sat at her vanity, her hairbrush in her hand, dressed in her nightclothes and a robe.

She gazed at him in the mirror, a smile curving her lips. "That was very heroic."

"What?"

"Running off those thugs."

She turned to face him, her eyes shining. He'd never seen her with that particular expression on her face. Was this the effect of the medicine? He stared at her, not sure what to make of her altered state.

She lifted her hand and waggled her finger at him. "But don't do it again. Not ever. Naughty Mr. Calhoun! I don't like bad men hurting my husband."

Her shoulders shook. She sniffed. "It..." her voice shook with emotion. "Upsets me greatly. I don't like blood. But I most especially don't like to see you hurt, Baron."

The words choked in her throat and tears rolled down her face. Baron wanted to offer a little levity, but he could see that any attempt at humor would fall flat. Emily was far too fragile this evening.

"A few years before she died, my mother had a... suitor who asked her to marry."

Baron drew a sharp breath. Emily's words startled him because he knew how much she disliked speaking about her mother. Part of him wanted to know more, and yet he felt an uncomfortable pang of remorse. It was hardly fair to listen to a person talk of her painful past when she was clearly under the influence of a sedating draught.

"Sweetheart-"

"She refu **Emily**

Emily woke in the early, pre-dawn darkness. It took her a moment to recall where she was. A hotel in San Antonio. She rubbed her eyes and tried to piece together the memories of the prior evening but couldn't summon any recollection of coming to bed.

Turning in her bed, she gazed out the window. In the distance, she could see the first hint of the sunrise. A ribbon of burnished crimson glowed, a stark contrast to the ebony sky. The stars faded, one by one as the first rays of sunlight gleamed, peeking over the horizon.

She rubbed her head, faintly aware of a dull throb behind her eyes. With a sigh, she recalled that Elizabeth and Henry were arriving that morning. She'd been looking forward to seeing her sister-in-law. Today was not a good day for a headache. Perhaps a cup of hot tea would revive her.

A soft growl greeted her ears. She drew a sharp breath. Had she imagined the sound? Slowly, she pushed up to a sitting position and searched the room for the source of the deep, masculine growl. In the dim light, she made out the shape of her husband, sprawled across the chesterfield.

Clapping a hand over her mouth, she fought the urge to cry out. Her heart crashed against her ribs. Her mouth went dry. Surely Baron hadn't slept in her room, had he?

She got out of bed and padded across the room, stopping a few paces from the chesterfield. He wore a light shirt and striped pajama pants. The chesterfield was about a foot too short for him and his bare feet rested on the floor. His expression, even in sleep, was a slight scowl, hinting at an uncomfortable night of sleep.

Turning away, she took care to tiptoe across the room in hopes she wouldn't wake him. She stepped into her dressing room and hastily donned one of her new frocks. Her mind reeled. Her hands shook. Why had he come to her room?

He'd always insisted on keeping his word. It disturbed her greatly to find him on the chesterfield, almost as much as being unable to remember the events of the night before.

When she finished dressing, she touched her lips, desperate to recall if she'd submitted to his demand of a kiss.

By the time she'd returned to the bedroom, the sun was up, and Baron had awakened. He smiled at her, his teeth flashing against the stubble that darkened his jaw. His expression was pure arrogance.

"Good morning, sweetheart. I'm glad you didn't scream when you saw me."

"What are you doing here?"

He scrubbed his hand down his face and sat up. "Do you remember what happened last night?"

She felt her blood chill in her veins. Unable to respond, she shook her head.

"We had a little run-in with a pair of ruffians. One of them had a knife."

Emily tried to comprehend his words. It was difficult to reconcile the terrifying notion with the way he smiled at her. When she didn't reply, he shrugged his shoulder carelessly. "You appeared to faint. I carried you up to the room and the hotel physician gave you something to settle your nerves."

Baron got to his feet and went to the door. "It was the doctor's recommendation that I stay near you. Otherwise I would have slept in my own room."

Wisps of memory drifted through her mind. She recalled the doctor coming. She recalled Baron arguing with him about attending to her without him present. And she recalled Baron had been hurt. He didn't seem to think that was worth mentioning, but Emily remembered seeing his injury. She bit her lip and swayed on her feet.

"Your arm," she whispered.

"None of that," Baron said with a stern tone. "I'm fine."

She let out a small murmur of surprise. He never spoke to her in that way. The dizziness faded, and she gave him a disapproving look.

"That's better," he muttered and left the room.

With a huff, she followed him to his room. "You can't fault me for fainting."

"I don't."

"I didn't do it on purpose."

"Of course not. Don't be ridiculous."

"Then why reproach me like I'm a child?"

"I didn't." He chuckled. "I told you to stop and you did."

She seethed at his words, mostly because he was right. How he'd managed to stop her from slipping into another bout of lightheadedness or maybe even a faint, she couldn't understand. He went into his room and pulled his shirt over his head. She gulped at the sight of him bare-chested. Her face flamed with mortification as she realized the effort it took to keep from admiring his powerful shoulders. She forced herself to keep her attention fixed above his smirking, infuriating mouth.

He held out his arm. "I had to have stitches last night, so you wouldn't have another spell in case you saw a drop of blood. I've been shot, stabbed and gotten scores of injuries when I was a bounty hunter. That was the first time I had *stitches*, thanks to you."

"You are the most impossible man I've ever met."

"You'd better toughen up, Emily. Life on a ranch isn't always a fairy tale. One day we'll have children and they'll skin their knees and bump their chins. They'll need a mother who can tend to them, not a mother who collapses in a heap."

She curled her hand into a fist but kept from shaking it at him like some sort of madwoman. "I thought you might even show me a tiny bit of sympathy. Last night you were all kind words and tenderness."

"You remember?"

"Y-yes. You spoke to me gently." She loosened the angry tension in her hands. "You were very kind. Now you're behaving as if I'm a badly-behaved brat."

He snorted, turned away and unwrapped the bandage around his arm. She let her gaze fall to the wound on his arm, noting the stitches. She recalled the blood from the night before but was too filled with indignation to feel the usual dizziness.

He went into his dressing room and emerged a moment later wearing trousers and a dress shirt. His shirt hung open, unbuttoned. Baron growled softly as he struggled with his cufflinks. Something about his displeasure made her own fade, and she smiled as she watched him attempt to affix the cufflinks.

"You seem to be having some trouble," she said lightly.

He glowered. "Yes, I'm in agony. Do you know anyone who could help me without fainting?"

She snickered and closed the distance between them. "I might be able to assist you, Mr. Calhoun."

"About time," he grumbled.

He gave her the cufflink and held out his arm. Standing so near him, so wonderfully close, made her thoughts spin, and not in the dizzying way she'd felt earlier. She let his masculine scent wash over her and tried to keep from letting her smile widen as she threaded the cufflinks through the buttonholes. She enjoyed the small, intimate act of helping him dress. She felt his gaze upon her as she moved to the other cuff. Neither of them spoke as she finished. Without moving away, she smiled up at him.

"Thank you, Emily."

"Of course."

She turned to leave but he set his hand on her arm to stop her.

"I need help with my buttons."

"Baron, please."

"It's true. I can't manage them on my own." He gave her a petulant look. "Please, Emily."

His tone was no longer sharp. The gentle request broke through her defenses. She eyed the buttons, wondering if he simply toyed with her or if he truly needed help. With a sudden flush of awareness, she realized she didn't care either way. She reveled at being near him and their repartee. Never before had she felt so at ease with a man. The notion surprised her, especially since he seemed so intent on provoking her.

She set her hands on the front of his shirt, noting his sharp inhale. She smoothed the fabric under her palm and began fastening the buttons, starting low and working her way up. As she moved up, she felt his gaze on her and sensed that he smiled.

"Baron," she said quietly. "You're an impossible man. One moment you're insulting me, the next you're asking me to help you with some absurd task. One I'm sure you could manage without me."

His smile faded. She wondered what she'd said to offend him. Her breath caught as she fastened the last button. Would he unleash a torrent of abuse for some perceived insult? Was he the sort of man whose moods changed with the wind? He didn't grow angry, however. If anything, he appeared pensive. His lids lowered as he regarded her with an intensity she hadn't seen before.

"I can't, Emily."

"You can't what?" she whispered.

"I can't manage without you."

Her breath caught. She retreated a few steps and turned to the door, suddenly anxious to gain some distance from him. Of all the things he might have said, *that* reply was the furthest from what she'd imagined. She paused in the doorway, fighting the swirl of emotions that churned inside her. He regarded her with a look of longing. It was too much. She fled his room.

A moment before, she'd fumed at his harsh tone. She realized now, that his tender words were far more dangerous than his words of reproach.

sed his offer of marriage. They quarreled. I heard them shouting. Our butler rushed in to try to stop them. He got hurt. There was blood everywhere."

"That's terrible. Did he... pass away?"

"No. But there was an inquiry, one that painted my mother in a bad light."

Baron grimaced. He wanted her to stop before she told him something she regretted. He should have kept her from telling him anything and prayed she would either forget about it or forgive him.

"Emily," he said gently. "You've had quite a shock. Come to bed."

To his surprise, she obeyed immediately. She set the brush aside, rose from the chair and went to him. He set his hand on her lower back and ushered her to the bed, drawing the blanket back for her. She slipped into the bed, resting against the pillows, closing her eyes.

"This medicine makes you as docile as a lamb," he said, unable to hold back a smile. "I might need to find the name of the draught."

"Baron," she whispered. "Don't tease me."

He stroked her hair, wishing more than anything he could wrap her in his arms. He eyed the side of the bed, imagined what it would feel like pulling Emily next to him and holding her throughout the night.

He hungered to be near her, to protect her from any bad memories of the night, but he knew he needed to wait. One day she'd give in to him, come to him willingly, and that sweet victory would be better than any stolen kiss.

"I'm afraid," she whispered.

He wrapped his hand around hers, lifted it and pressed it against his jaw. "Don't be afraid, Emily. I'll watch over you. I'm going to sleep on the chesterfield here in your room. If you need me sometime during the night, I'll be right here. Just call my name."

She sighed. "Good night, Baron."

Chapter Twenty-One

Emily

Emily woke in the early, pre-dawn darkness. It took her a moment to recall where she was. A hotel in San Antonio. She rubbed her eyes and tried to piece together the memories of the prior evening but couldn't summon any recollection of coming to bed.

Turning in her bed, she gazed out the window. In the distance, she could see the first hint of the sunrise. A ribbon of burnished crimson glowed, a stark contrast to the ebony sky. The stars faded, one by one as the first rays of sunlight gleamed, peeking over the horizon.

She rubbed her head, faintly aware of a dull throb behind her eyes. With a sigh, she recalled that Elizabeth and Henry were arriving that morning. She'd been looking forward to seeing her sister-in-law. Today was not a good day for a headache. Perhaps a cup of hot tea would revive her.

A soft growl greeted her ears. She drew a sharp breath. Had she imagined the sound? Slowly, she pushed up to a sitting position and searched the room for the source of the deep, masculine growl. In the dim light, she made out the shape of her husband, sprawled across the chesterfield.

Clapping a hand over her mouth, she fought the urge to cry out. Her heart crashed against her ribs. Her mouth went dry. Surely Baron hadn't slept in her room, had he?

She got out of bed and padded across the room, stopping a few paces from the chesterfield. He wore a light shirt and striped pajama pants. The chesterfield was about a foot too short for him and his bare feet rested on the floor. His expression, even in sleep, was a slight scowl, hinting at an uncomfortable night of sleep.

Turning away, she took care to tiptoe across the room in hopes she wouldn't wake him. She stepped into her dressing room and hastily donned one of her new frocks. Her mind reeled. Her hands shook. Why had he come to her room?

He'd always insisted on keeping his word. It disturbed her greatly to find him on the chesterfield, almost as much as being unable to remember the events of the night before. When she finished dressing, she touched her lips, desperate to recall if she'd submitted to his demand of a kiss.

By the time she'd returned to the bedroom, the sun was up, and Baron had awakened. He smiled at her, his teeth flashing against the stubble that darkened his jaw. His expression was pure arrogance.

"Good morning, sweetheart. I'm glad you didn't scream when you saw me."

"What are you doing here?"

He scrubbed his hand down his face and sat up. "Do you remember what happened last night?"

She felt her blood chill in her veins. Unable to respond, she shook her head.

"We had a little run-in with a pair of ruffians. One of them had a knife."

Emily tried to comprehend his words. It was difficult to reconcile the terrifying notion with the way he smiled at her. When she didn't reply, he shrugged his shoulder carelessly.

"You appeared to faint. I carried you up to the room and the hotel physician gave you something to settle your nerves."

Baron got to his feet and went to the door. "It was the doctor's recommendation that I stay near you. Otherwise, I would have slept in my own room."

Wisps of memory drifted through her mind. She recalled the doctor coming. She recalled Baron arguing with him about attending to her without him present. And she recalled Baron had been hurt. He didn't seem to think that was worth mentioning, but Emily remembered seeing his injury. She bit her lip and swayed on her feet.

"Your arm," she whispered.

"None of that," Baron said with a stern tone. "I'm fine."

She let out a small murmur of surprise. He never spoke to her in that way. The dizziness faded, and she gave him a disapproving look.

"That's better," he muttered and left the room.

With a huff, she followed him to his room. "You can't fault me for fainting."

"I don't."

"I didn't do it on purpose."

"Of course not. Don't be ridiculous."

"Then why reproach me like I'm a child?"

"I didn't." He chuckled. "I told you to stop and you did."

She seethed at his words, mostly because he was right. How he'd managed to stop her from slipping into another bout of lightheadedness or maybe even a faint, she couldn't understand. He went into his room and pulled his shirt over his head. She gulped at the sight of him bare-chested. Her face flamed with mortification as she realized the effort it took to keep from admiring his powerful shoulders. She forced herself to keep her attention fixed above his smirking, infuriating mouth.

He held out his arm. "I had to have stitches last night, so you wouldn't have another spell in case you saw a drop of blood. I've been shot, stabbed and gotten scores of injuries when I was a bounty hunter. That was the first time I had *stitches*, thanks to you."

"You are the most impossible man I've ever met."

"You'd better toughen up, Emily. Life on a ranch isn't always a fairy tale. One day we'll have children and they'll skin their knees and bump their chins. They'll need a mother who can tend to them, not a mother who collapses in a heap."

She curled her hand into a fist but kept from shaking it at him like some sort of madwoman. "I thought you might even show me a tiny bit of sympathy. Last night you were all kind words and tenderness."

"You remember?"

"Y-yes. You spoke to me gently." She loosened the angry tension in her hands. "You were very kind. Now you're behaving as if I'm a badly-behaved brat."

He snorted, turned away and unwrapped the bandage around his arm. She let her gaze fall to the wound on his arm, noting the stitches. She recalled the blood from the night before but was too filled with indignation to feel the usual dizziness.

He went into his dressing room and emerged a moment later wearing trousers and a dress shirt. His shirt hung open, unbuttoned. Baron growled softly as he struggled with his cufflinks. Something about his displeasure made her own fade, and she smiled as she watched him attempt to affix the cufflinks.

"You seem to be having some trouble," she said lightly.

He glowered. "Yes, I'm in agony. Do you know anyone who could help me without fainting?"

She snickered and closed the distance between them. "I might be able to assist you, Mr. Calhoun."

"About time," he grumbled.

He gave her the cufflink and held out his arm. Standing so near him, so wonderfully close, made her thoughts spin, and not in the dizzying way she'd felt earlier. She let his masculine scent wash over her and tried to keep from letting her smile widen as she threaded the cufflinks through the buttonholes. She enjoyed the small, intimate act of helping him dress. She felt his gaze upon her as she moved to the other cuff. Neither of them spoke as she finished. Without moving away, she smiled up at him.

"Thank you, Emily."

"Of course."

She turned to leave but he set his hand on her arm to stop her.

"I need help with my buttons."

"Baron, please."

"It's true. I can't manage them on my own." He gave her a petulant look. "Please, Emily."

His tone was no longer sharp. The gentle request broke through her defenses. She eyed the buttons, wondering if he simply toyed with her or if he truly needed help. With a sudden flush of awareness, she realized she didn't care either way. She reveled at being near him and their repartee. Never before had she felt so at ease with a man. The notion surprised her, especially since he seemed so intent on provoking her.

She set her hands on the front of his shirt, noting his sharp inhale. She smoothed the fabric under her palm and began fastening the buttons, starting low and working her way up.

As she moved up, she felt his gaze on her and sensed that he smiled.

"Baron," she said quietly. "You're an impossible man. One moment you're insulting me, the next you're asking me to help you with some absurd task. One I'm sure you could manage without me."

His smile faded. She wondered what she'd said to offend him. Her breath caught as she fastened the last button. Would he unleash a torrent of abuse for some perceived insult? Was he the sort of man whose moods changed with the wind? He didn't grow angry, however. If anything, he appeared pensive. His lids lowered as he regarded her with an intensity she hadn't seen before.

"I can't, Emily."

"You can't what?" she whispered.

"I can't manage without you."

Her breath caught. She retreated a few steps and turned to the door, suddenly anxious to gain some distance from him. Of all the things he might have said, *that* reply was the furthest from what she'd imagined. She paused in the doorway, fighting the swirl of emotions that churned inside her. He regarded her with a look of longing. It was too much. She fled his room.

A moment before, she'd fumed at his harsh tone. She realized now that his tender words were far more dangerous than his words of reproach.

Chapter Twenty-Two

Baron

Baron eyed Elizabeth and Henry with surprise as they walked through the park. His sister and brother-in-law held hands and exchanged whispers. Elizabeth giggled at something Henry said. A moment later, Elizabeth made her husband blush.

Emily noticed their antics too and gave him a bewildered look.

"They look more like newlyweds than we do," Baron grumbled.

His wife pressed her lips together and looked away. He hadn't intended to hurt her feelings, but it was undeniable. Henry and Elizabeth were enjoying a sweet, flirtatious moment. He envied them.

"This is all on account of your drawing," he said under his breath.

"What does that mean?"

"You drew such a pretty picture of Elizabeth, you've revived their marriage."

Emily's lips parted with surprise and then slowly curved into a smile. "You think that's what's happened?"

Baron shrugged. "They never argued. They just lived apart in a way. It was very hard on my sister when the doctors told her she couldn't have children."

"What are you talking about?" Elizabeth called over her shoulder.

"Just that you and Henry seem quite happy with each other," Baron said.

"Pooh! We've always been happy with each other," she sputtered. "Isn't that so, Henry?"

Henry stopped. Arm-in-arm with her husband, Elizabeth was obliged to stop as well.

"Elizabeth and I have always gotten along very well, Baron. Your sister is the love of my life."

"You see what I mean?" Baron muttered.

"Yes, dear," Emily whispered.

Baron chuckled.

Elizabeth clicked her tongue. "You two are poking fun at us, aren't you?"

"Maybe a little," Baron replied. He gestured to a stately building on the edge of the park. "Let me make it up to you by taking you to lunch at the Breckenridge Tea Room, the pride of San Antonio."

They ascended the stone steps. Doormen opened the doors for them and the group was ushered to a table in a quiet corner overlooking a private terrace with fountains. Waiters brought tea and an array of fancy foods.

A gentleman came to the table, a young man who Baron introduced as David Whittier. Everyone said a polite hello, all except Emily. Baron watched Emily grow pale, her eyes downcast. David congratulated her and Baron on their nuptials, but Emily remained silent.

"Thank you," Baron said, covering her hand with his to offer some reassurance.

David frowned but recovered quickly, muttered a few comments about looking forward to the meeting of Presidio investors in a few days. He excused himself from the group and returned to his lunch party on the other side of the salon.

Baron arched his brow and gave her a questioning look. Emily shook her head as though wanting to fend off any questions. The waiters served a hot consommé, followed by an endive salad. Emily merely picked at her food.

As the meal drew to a close, Baron leaned over to ask if she wanted to return to the hotel to rest. Elizabeth must have sensed something was wrong. She shook her head and gave Emily a sympathetic look.

"Are you feeling poorly, dear?"

"A little light-headed," Emily said. "I fainted last night."

"What?" Elizabeth demanded, looking at Baron in horror.

"I wasn't going to mention anything," he said. He studied Emily, wondering why she would tell Henry and Elizabeth anything about last night. She had to know that Elizabeth would panic at the first hint of danger. What was more, he wondered why Emily trembled. Ever since David had stopped by the table, she'd grown quiet and pale.

"What happened?" Elizabeth demanded.

Baron sighed. "We had a run-in with a couple of rough men yesterday evening. They wanted to cause us trouble. I sent them on their way."

"Really?" Elizabeth frowned. Baron heard the skepticism in her voice.

"One of them cut Baron with a knife," Emily blurted.

Elizabeth gasped. Her hand flew to her heart. Even Henry gave a cry of dismay. Baron stifled a growl. Later, when they were alone in their room, he'd have to have a talk with Emily and explain that she needed to keep some things to herself.

The rest of the meal was spent dissecting the events of the evening before. It soon became clear that both Elizabeth and

Henry blamed him for putting Emily in the path of danger even though he'd kept the men far from her. He rubbed the back of his neck wondering how long he'd have to listen to his sister's lectures about taking care of Emily.

A long, long time. He was certain. Elizabeth would stay on the topic the way a bloodhound tracked a scent.

"I don't care for San Antonio," Emily said, her color returning somewhat. "Perhaps I can travel back to Magnolia with Elizabeth and Henry. You can manage without me, can't you?"

Elizabeth beamed. "That would be lovely, dear. I've missed you so, even more than I've missed my brother. It's lovely having another woman to talk to."

Baron gritted his teeth. Why did Emily want to leave? He felt certain it had nothing to do with the events of the night before. He ignored his sister and gave Emily a hard look, hoping she'd drop the subject.

Elizabeth spoke. "Oh, come, Baron. It can't be any fun for a young woman to traipse around with you to your meetings. The poor dear."

Emily nodded. "It's dreadfully dull."

Baron narrowed his eyes. "We're going to discuss this when we get back to the hotel. Privately."

Elizabeth pouted and offered long, weary sighs for the rest of the lunch. Henry looked as bewildered as Baron felt, and Emily tried her best to avoid his gaze. Once lunch was over, Baron paid the bill. He ushered his family back to the hotel, eager to get Emily to himself so he could get to the bottom of her scheme to leave with Elizabeth.

As they walked through the park, making their way back to the hotel, Emily paired up with Elizabeth, leaving Baron to walk with Henry.

"Marriage can be a challenge the first few months," Henry offered.

"That's not a good reason to be apart."

"Perhaps Emily has some questions about her role as your wife."

Baron snorted. "Doubtful. She and I have a marriage of convenience."

Henry stopped in his tracks and gaped at Baron. His eyes grew as round as plums. "Whatever you do, don't tell Elizabeth. She'll be heartbroken if you and Emily don't have a family. Heartbroken. I thought you wanted an heir."

"Of course, I want an heir. I want a wife in every sense of the word too, but I had to promise Emily to keep my distance. I'd hoped, over time, I'd charm her into forgetting the convenience part."

Henry's mouth tilted into a smile. His smile widened. He chuckled. Soon his laughter brought tears to his eyes and he was obliged to wipe them with his handkerchief.

Baron waited for him to compose himself. The women walked ahead, arm-in-arm, neither of them noticing that the men had stopped. His shoulders knotted with tension and his hands curled into fists as he fought a wave of irritation.

"Henry, you're usually more helpful. What's so amusing?"

"*You* are amusing!" Henry's voice rasped with the effort of suppressing his laughter. "You planned on *charming* her? When have you, Baron Calhoun, ever charmed anyone?"

Baron felt a tug of self-consciousness, suddenly aware of how he must have appeared, fists clenched, glowering at his brother-in-law, a man of the cloth who stood a head shorter. He probably looked like a brute. He checked to see if the women were watching the spectacle, but they walked ahead, deep in conversation, unaware of anything behind them.

Henry's laughter subsided.

"I could charm my wife," Baron said. "I could."

Henry waved a dismissive hand. "Give her time. She's young. Let her spend some time with Elizabeth so she can have her fill of feminine conversation."

"I don't want her to have her fill of feminine conversation," Baron said.

Henry shrugged. "I'm not surprised. Do it your way."

"I can't be parted from her." Baron cast a longing gaze his wife's direction just as she turned the corner with Elizabeth. "I *won't* be parted from her."

Henry groaned. "Eh, fine. Nobody listens to me. Why is that?"

Baron stared at the end of the pathway where Emily had just walked a moment before. He smiled at the way her skirts had fluttered in the breeze and the way she'd looped her arm around Elizabeth. A soft warmth of longing seeped through his heart. He yearned to catch up to Elizabeth and Emily, to gather his wife close and tuck her under his arm.

"I listen to you, Henry," he said. "But I'll still do things in my own way."

Henry grumbled. "And where have I heard *that* before?"

Chapter Twenty-Three

Emily

That afternoon, she tried her best to talk Baron into agreeing to let her go back to Magnolia with Henry and Elizabeth. Elizabeth tried her best to convince her brother too, but it seemed the more they tried to prevail, the more he resisted.

As they prepared to meet Elizabeth and Henry for dinner, she implored him again. "I enjoyed seeing the building you intended to buy. It was just a small group. Your meeting with the cartel will be different. It might be as many as what, a dozen businessmen?"

"I don't know. What difference does it make? You'll be with me. You'll be wonderful. I like the idea of having you on my arm, and I want to know your thoughts."

Emily wrung her hands, wondering who would attend the meeting. Maybe it was nothing more than a mere coincidence that the man who stopped at their table was a Whittier. Or maybe David was Orson's son. She tried to soothe her concerns by telling herself Whittier was likely a common name in this part of Texas.

"Besides," Baron held up his injured arm, "I might need your assistance."

Her face warmed with embarrassment. He noted her dismay and gave her a playful smile. Her fretfulness grew as she envisioned a disastrous meeting with the other businessmen where one of them would notice the curious shade of her eyes and denounce her in front of everyone, and worst of all in front of Baron.

"I don't want to disappoint you," she said, her voice choked with emotion. "I don't want to cause you shame."

She lifted her hand to her lips, wishing she hadn't been so hasty. Her eyes prickled. Her breath lodged in her chest, weighing as much as an iron anvil.

His smile vanished. He crossed the room, stopping a few steps away from her, a furious look darkening his eyes. "Don't say that, Emily. You could never disappoint me."

She retreated a step to put some space between them.

"I wake up every morning, thanking God that I'm married to you. How could I be ashamed of you? I love you."

She heard a small, fragile cry. It took a moment to realize it had come from her own lips. "All right."

Cringing, she wondered if she could possibly have said anything more absurd. She saw the pain her response caused as he pressed his lips together. He crossed his arms across his chest and studied her with a cooler expression.

"I don't expect you to love me back," he said. "I know I forced your hand when I asked you to marry me."

"It's not that, Baron."

"You don't need to tell me. I'll find out more about you as time passes."

She bit her lip.

"And you'll find out more about me, too." He shrugged and turned away. "This meeting is very important to me. After I finish my business with the cartel, I'll take you to California to show you the ocean."

There was little more to say, not without revealing the source of her worry. To explain her feelings to him would be to tell him about her life before she came to Magnolia. She couldn't bear to explain the filthy details of her mother's plan. If he knew, he'd never see her in the same light. He'd regret taking her as his wife and might even tell Elizabeth and Henry about her past.

Later, as she took his arm to walk down to the hotel dining room, she recalled his words, playing them over in her mind, again and again.

I love you... I don't expect you to love me back...

They dined in the elegant dining room, sitting by a roaring fire while Henry told stories about working as a missionary in Mexico. Emily only heard half of what he said. She tried to eat the filet Baron had ordered for her, but nothing tasted good.

"What is it, Emily?" Elizabeth asked. "Still not feeling well?"

"Not especially."

"Is your stomach queasy?" she asked with a gleam in her eye. "Can I hope my prayers for a little one might finally be answered?"

Henry coughed and took a gulp of his drink. "Darling – don't embarrass the poor girl."

Emily blushed and looked at Baron for help, but he merely smiled in response. He seemed to be enjoying her discomfort. Probably retaliation for asking to go back to Magnolia with Henry and Elizabeth, or perhaps a little revenge for not responding when he told her he loved her.

"I'm certain we don't have news of a little one," Emily said softly.

"Let's have dessert," Henry said a little too loudly. "Anyone?"

Emily smiled at Henry's attempt to change the conversation.

Elizabeth eyed her plate. "You hardly touched your dinner. Would you mind terribly if I sampled a little of your steak?"

Baron chuckled. "Elizabeth, you don't usually have such a prodigious appetite."

"Don't be rude," his sister snapped. She set her empty plate aside and motioned for Emily to hand over her plate.

"Is it just me," Baron asked, turning to Henry, "or is my sister's dress a little snug?"

"Horrid man," Elizabeth muttered. "Forty wonders you've managed this long with him, Emily. You really should come home with us."

Henry chuckled, but quieted when Elizabeth shot him a look of outrage.

"Her dress isn't snug at all," he hurried to say. "Elizabeth is the same girlish bride I married fifteen years ago."

Elizabeth gazed at her husband and sighed. "And you are the same handsome and charming young man I married so many years ago."

Henry blushed, took Elizabeth's hand and kissed it.

Emily couldn't help but smile at the sweet display of affection. Baron, she noticed, watched the interaction between Henry and Elizabeth with a slightly bewildered expression.

Later, when they'd returned to the room, he asked her what she knew. "Did Elizabeth say anything to you?"

Emily sat on the chaise in the sitting room and unbuckled her boots. They were elegant but not the most comfortable. She sighed a breath of relief as she slipped them from her feet.

"She didn't say anything, but she did seem almost..." Emily rubbed her instep and winced at the discomfort. "I don't know. Giddy perhaps."

Baron sat down on the chesterfield on the other side of her. He reached down, grasped her feet in his hands and lifted them to his lap. Before she could protest, he waved off her concerns.

"Hush. Let me take care of you."

His hands on her feet felt unbearably familiar and close despite the thin barrier of her sensible stockings. He didn't touch her directly. No, that would have been too much. Still, this felt far too intimate. She tried to pull away, but he soothed her with gentle words. He rubbed her feet with a touch that was firm enough to ease the ache but wasn't too firm to cause her more discomfort.

"The two of them seem quite in love," Baron mused.

"Maybe it's..." Emily let her words die away as she recalled the conversation she'd had with Elizabeth.

"What?" Baron asked softly, smiling at her. "Tell me their secret so I can charm my reluctant bride."

She laughed at his endearing words. "There's no secret. Elizabeth says Henry is taken with the picture I drew of her. He says he'd spent too many years hardly noticing how lovely his wife is." Emily blushed. "He told her that my picture reminded him of why he fell in love with her so many years ago."

Holding her breath, she waited for him to say something dismissive or cynical. Instead, he nodded. The look in his eyes softened as he gazed at her.

Emily shook her head. "I'm sure she's just being kind."

Baron snorted. "Elizabeth? Doubtful."

She let herself enjoy the moment. His touch and his gaze unraveled the hard knot inside her chest and she would have liked to stay near him, enjoying their conversation. In the back of her mind, she fretted about what tomorrow might bring, imagining every single demon from her past. She'd stand before him, humiliated and called out. Worse, she'd ruin his chance to invest in the cartel.

"I don't want to go tomorrow, Baron."

He nodded. "Joining the cartel is important to me. Very important. It's everything I've worked for. I want you there by my side."

Her heart thudded, heavy and hard against her chest. His tone was gentle, and his eyes held her in his gaze, making her breath catch. How could she refuse him?

Chapter Twenty-Four

Baron

With a weary sigh, Baron watched Emily and Elizabeth embrace for what had to be the fifth time. Henry stood by the buggy, waiting for his wife, a bemused smile lighting his expression. The man was still smitten with this wife after how many years?

Baron hoped his and Emily's happiness would also last years and years. Of course, that would mean he'd have to coax her into falling in love with him to begin with. Her pinched expression, the worry etched across her brow, told him he was failing that task. The reproach in her eyes showed him just how much she wished she could return to Magnolia with Elizabeth and Henry.

He'd refused her request. And he'd refuse her again if she asked. She might think he was an unfeeling brute, but he'd argue that he yearned for her company because he cared for her. He loved her. He'd said as much to her the night before.

Did that make him selfish?

Maybe.

He demanded she stay with him because he was in love with her. His chest filled with a hard, heavy weight as he watched her say her final goodbye. He was afraid to lose her. If he sent her off with Elizabeth and Henry, she might steal away and leave him. He'd done nothing to deserve her love. What if she decided that marriage to him was intolerable?

"Good bye, Baron," Elizabeth called.

"Please. Go already," Baron muttered. He pasted a smile to his lips and waved from the steps. He'd already wished her safe travels, thanked her for coming, told her to take good care of herself and Henry too. What else could he say?

Thankfully, Henry and Elizabeth climbed into the buggy and a moment later set off for Magnolia. Emily turned to face him and gave him an awkward smile. When had his sweet, sassy bride become reticent? Did she fret about his joining the cartel? Or was it him?

A buggy waited to take them to a lunch reception. He walked down the steps and gestured to the black, one-horse gig. "It's time for us to go."

She nodded but seemed to grow more pale. He helped her into the buggy and closed the door behind them. The driver put the horse into a trot and they began their journey.

"The lunch is being held at the ranch of the late Orson Whittier."

Emily looked away. "I understand he owned a number of the cartel's mines."

Baron wondered how she knew that about Whittier but realized that she must have read the reports he'd received. Another reason he wanted her by his side. Her sharp, inquisitive mind intrigued him. He considered himself very lucky to have a wife who was both bright and beautiful.

"He did," Baron said. "When he passed away, he left a number of debts. His son had to sell a great deal of property to pay his creditors."

"What a shame."

Emily's tone sounded bitter. He noticed that she often seemed to regard wealthy people with disdain. Why would she? His wife was a mystery to him at times and her reserve always made him uneasy.

For the rest of the trip neither of them spoke. They arrived at the sprawling ranch house just as a light mist began to fall. Ranch hands came to the buggy with umbrellas and escorted them inside. Baron kept a protective arm around Emily as they passed through the front door. They were shown into the parlor where a blaze crackled in an immense fireplace.

The group, composed mostly of wealthy ranchers, gathered in small clusters, discussing cattle prices, the railroads and land grants. Baron recognized a few of the men, but not all. When he entered the parlor, the conversation seemed to quiet down as the men regarded him with curiosity. The attention filled him with a certain amount of pride. He'd worked hard to get to this point in his life. He had more money than all these men combined and could make or break the Presidio Cartel if he decided to invest his money in the group.

Charles Stanton, standing on the far side of the room, smiled when he saw him and came to his side.

"Baron, excellent to see you. I worried that the rain might keep you from joining us."

"I had to come, Charles. I'm the reason for your meeting."

Emily drew a sharp breath at his arrogant tone, but he ignored her. This was the way it was when men talked about prospects. The group wanted his money. He wanted to invest. But none of them would act as if they wanted anything at all.

Charles laughed. "It's true. You are the reason we're here." He turned to Emily. "Mrs. Calhoun, it's a pleasure to meet you."

Emily offered her hand. Charles shook it politely.

"The pleasure is mine," she replied, sounding anything but pleased.

"There are a few ladies here," Charles went on to say. "Perhaps you'd like to join them."

Emily's hold on his arm tightened. She hadn't anticipated being apart from him, and he hadn't thought about the likelihood that the ladies would convene separately.

"The men are going to visit the mine that the Whittier family just reopened. We were forced to close after an accident last month. A nuisance, really, but that's what happens when a few miners die. It's just a short ride from here. We're eager for Baron to see the operations. The ladies, of course, won't join us, but we'll eat lunch together in the dining room. Mrs. Whittier always provides a lovely meal."

Emily didn't reply. Instead, she stared at Charles as if he'd grown another pair of ears. She looked stunned. Charles blinked and looked back and forth between Baron and Emily.

"Sweetheart," Baron said, turning her to face him. "We won't be long."

"I didn't know..." her words faded.

"You didn't know what?"

"I didn't know we'd be apart. I don't care for that, particularly. I also didn't think you'd actually enter the mine."

Her voice trembled as she turned her attention back to Charles. "Why does he have to go into the mine?"

Charles colored. "He doesn't have to do anything. I would never attempt to give Baron directions."

Baron felt the men watching with interest. Women didn't express opinions on the matters of men. While he usually sought his wife's opinion, this was more than he'd anticipated or enjoyed. He suppressed a growl.

"Why don't you excuse us, Charles, while I escort my wife to chat with the ladies."

They walked through the house, a servant leading them to where the women convened without their husbands. He sensed Emily's dismay growing with every step. When they reached the door, he paused, dismissed the servant and took Emily's hands in his.

"Why do you get to say when I come and when I go?" she demanded. "But I'm not allowed the same privilege?"

"Emily," he said sharply. "I cannot invest in a venture that I don't know anything about."

"Then don't invest. Fifteen men died in a nearby mine last month. I read those reports you received. Fifteen families without their husbands, brothers or fathers."

"Nothing's going to happen to me." He shrugged. "If it does, you'll be a rich widow."

She recoiled, fury blazing in her eyes.

"Why, Emily," he said softly, turning to leave. "You *do* care."

Chapter Twenty-Five

Emily

Emily managed to compose herself as she entered the parlor. She hadn't ever seen that cool, detached side of Baron and it bothered her more than she could say. Rich widow indeed! He was a beast for saying something so heartless to her. She turned over a few comments she'd like to share with him later that evening. She'd give him a piece of her mind.

Stepping into the parlor, she was surprised to find just a mere handful of ladies. She'd expected to find a large group of women in the parlor, but there were only four. One woman, older and dressed in black, met her at the door and introduced herself as Virginia Whittier. A spry, energetic lady with a quick smile.

Orson's widow.

Emily felt the blood drain from her face and half-expected the woman to set upon her with ugly words and accusations. Again, she felt her resentment burn. Baron had brought her to the Whittier house and promptly abandoned her with people she didn't know. Like Mrs. Whittier.

Emily braced herself for the onslaught. To her surprise, Mrs. Whittier gave her a friendly smile. "I saw you when you arrived," Mrs. Whittier said. "I watched from the window."

Emily swallowed hard, trying to dislodge the lump in her throat. She wished she could run from the room, find Baron and beg to stay with him even if it meant visiting the dreaded mine. Anything was better than coming face-to-face with Orson Whittier's widow.

"Don't you want to know why I watched, Emily?"

After a long moment, Emily found her voice. "If you care to tell me, Mrs. Whittier, I'd be pleased to know."

"Call me Virginia. I wanted to see the girl who won the heart of Baron Calhoun." Her lips quirked. She glanced to where the three other women sat, sipping tea. "Katherine Stanton would like to scratch out your lovely, violet eyes."

Emily let out a huff of surprise. She studied the woman Virginia had referred to, an elegant blonde. The young lady stared at Emily from across the room, giving her an icy gaze. Emily shook her head, not comprehending anything Virginia was saying. Who on earth was Katherine Stanton? Obviously, some kin to Charles, the man she'd just met, but why would the woman have any ill wishes towards her?

Virginia sighed. "My husband, Orson, died three and a half months ago. I've been in mourning since then. Well, mostly pretending to be in mourning. It's a dull formality. I can't attend any parties. I'm expected to wear black all the time and black makes me look old and drab, don't you think?"

Emily held her breath, not entirely sure which direction the conversation might go. Was Virginia Whittier mad?

"N-no, I don't think you look old or drab."

Virginia waved a dismissive hand. "Oh, stop."

"Why does that woman want to scratch my eyes out?" Emily asked.

Virginia chuckled. "She fully expected Baron Calhoun to offer for her."

Katherine Stanton... the memory of Elizabeth talking about Baron's sweetheart came flooding back into her mind. She recalled working on Henry's watch, trying to keep her hands from shaking as Elizabeth fretted about Baron not offering for the girl.

"All I've heard for the last hour is how a mere shop girl stole her fiancé." Virginia's eyes sparkled. "You naughty girl, stealing poor Katherine's fellow away."

The woman sitting across from Katherine turned to give Emily a cold stare.

Virginia went on, in a low, conspiratorial tone. "There's the heartbroken mother. The *almost* mother-in-law. She's a delight, let me tell you. Even better than my Ozzie's mother, my dear, sweet, horrible mother-in-law."

Her words startled Emily more than anything else she'd said. The stark reality crashed through Emily's mind. She stood in the home of the man who had paid for her schooling. For years, he'd groomed her to become his mistress. If she hadn't undermined his plans, she would have indeed become *Ozzie's* mistress. What choice would she have had? None.

Virginia frowned. "Don't look so stricken, darling. I won't let them hurt you."

"Thank you," Emily said softly.

Virginia took her elbow and led her to where the ladies sat, gesturing for her to sit on one end of the chaise as she took the other. She introduced Emily to the two Stanton ladies. Another woman sat quietly, her hands folded in her lap.

"And this trembling wallflower is Sarah Hughes," Virginia said. "My secretary."

Emily eyed her, noting her modest dress and unassuming demeanor. If Katherine Stanton was the embodiment of privilege and entitlement, Sarah seemed to be the picture of a shy and gentle-natured young woman.

"Isn't this lovely?" Virginia took a sip of her tea. "What shall we talk about?"

Mrs. Stanton gave her a brittle smile. "My husband speaks highly of your son, David."

Virginia's expression softened, giving way to a look of maternal pride. She glanced at Sarah, her lips tugging into a smile as she set her tea down. "What can I say about my son other than he's nothing at all like his father."

Mrs. Stanton and her daughter exchanged bewildered looks while Sarah kept her gaze averted. Emily felt a pang of sympathy for the quiet girl. She wondered why Virginia might want to treat Sarah unkindly and felt a small wave of gratitude that the woman didn't know anything about her own past. Virginia Whittier was not a woman to be trifled with.

"My father says he's a hard worker," Katherine said.

Virginia nodded. "David is a hard worker because he has no choice. His father squandered a great deal of money, my money. If David wishes to marry, he'll have to recoup at least part of it."

"How long will that take?" Mrs. Stanton asked.

Virginia's smile widened. She was enjoying herself immensely. She refilled her teacup, poured a cup for Emily and chatted about the Whittier family fortunes. Both Stanton women listened, taking in every word like hungry little sparrows.

Jealousy twisted inside Emily's heart as she regarded Katherine. She could see why Baron might have liked the girl. She was blonde and elegant and most importantly, she hadn't been raised to be a man's mistress. The girl wasn't above flaunting her assets, however. Her neckline dipped, almost indecently, to show off her generous curves.

Emily didn't dwell on the sight of Katherine for long. The weight of her predicament felt like a pall stretched over her heart. She clung to the shred of hope that no one would discover her identity, but she still yearned to leave Whittier Ranch, to put it behind her and never come back. Mrs. Whittier clearly didn't miss her husband, but she probably wouldn't take kindly to Emily being there in her home if she knew anything about her past.

Emily watched Virginia Whittier toy with the Stanton women, suggesting that David might be looking for a wife when he had the means. She was a shrewd woman. That much was clear.

Sarah, the other young girl, looked more miserable with each passing moment. Twice, she excused herself from the group and wandered to the window. She peered out, searching. The first time she did that, Emily hadn't paid much attention, but the second time, it dawned on her that Sarah looked for David Whittier. The girl was in love with Virginia's son.

"Tell me, Katherine, dear," Virginia said. "Do you believe in true love?"

Katherine blinked in confusion. "I suppose it happens."

Virginia looked wistful. "It didn't happen to me. Maybe that's why I'd like very much to see my son find true love."

Katherine jerked her head to face her mother. "Well... I don't know. What do you think, Mother? Is there such a thing?"

"Yes," her mother replied, slowly, choosing her words carefully. "I believe it's possible."

"What about fate?" Virginia asked.

Katherine furrowed her brow. "I don't believe in fate. I believe in two people coming together to form a mutually agreeable relationship. Marriage is about choosing well. A woman has to be careful."

Katherine swept her gaze towards Emily, her lip curling. "She shouldn't marry beneath herself, but she shouldn't overreach either. It's bad manners."

Emily hid her smile behind her teacup, not deigning to reply to the spiteful comments.

Virginia sighed. "That's just what Sarah likes to say. Isn't it, dear?"

Sarah looked as alarmed as a small creature cornered by a pack of wild animals. She looked around the room, her face coloring as she bit her lip. Silence stretched between them as Virginia deliberately waited for her response.

"I only turned eighteen, Mrs. Whittier." Her voice trembled.

Virginia scoffed. "What does that have to do with the price of tea in China?"

"I'm not r-ready for marriage."

Virginia laughed mischievously.

"There, there, Sarah," Mrs. Stanton said, coming to the girl's rescue. "You'll marry one day. Maybe a nice postal worker."

"That's right," Katherine chimed in. "Maybe a street sweeper."

At that, Virginia laughed heartily. "She won't marry either, if I have anything to say about matters."

Katherine and her mother both shook their heads in confusion.

"The course of true love," Virginia said, coyly, "sometimes needs a little help from a meddling old woman."

Emily almost smiled at Virginia's words. A dull pain ached in her chest as she thought of the notion of true love. She was still a newlywed yet had never felt so far from true love.

The rain drummed on the windows, coming down harder. The dark skies cast a grim light across the study. Emily's spirits sank as she imagined the men heading to the mine in the downpour. Surely, they wouldn't descend into the mineshaft, not with the deluge. She said a silent prayer, asking the Lord to watch over the men and bring them home safe.

Chapter Twenty-Six

Baron

Three buckboards pulled by draft horses took the men to the mine entrance. Several men passed a bottle of spirits around, but Baron declined. Charles Stanton, he noticed, drank more than his share and grew louder as the journey progressed.

Baron sat beside David at the front of the lead buckboard.

"I can't stand the likes of men like Charles Stanton," David said. "I'm sorry. I know he's a friend of yours."

Baron shrugged. "We're friends, but that doesn't mean I admire him getting drunk. I've never seen him like this."

Baron recalled Charles's words about his wife and daughter. They quarreled endlessly, making his life a misery, he claimed. Maybe that was why the man was so eager to knock back a few belts of whatever they passed around.

The arguments died down when a few of the men broke out into song.

David shook his head. "Not one of them is going to be fit to take a look at the mine."

They drove through a valley, along the bank of a broad stream. A mare and foal stood under an oak tree at the water's edge. The two horses were a matched pair, pintos with the prettiest markings Baron had ever seen.

"Good looking horses," Baron commented.

"That foal came along last week. She's part of my mustang herd. The rest of the herd has got to be nearby. The mares don't like to take the new foals around the herd for a few weeks."

Baron raised his hand. "Hold up just a minute."

David stopped the horses, so Baron could admire the animals.

"Do you break them?"

David shook his head. "If I tried, they'd break me. They're as wild as can be and I like it that way. I give them the run of this part of the ranch."

The foal watched them, his ears pricked forward, but grew bored after a moment. He nuzzled his mother. She sniffed his head. Despite the rain, Baron heard the mare whicker softly. Beneath the oak, the mother and foal were sheltered from much of the downpour.

A twinge of longing came over him as he admired the horses. He wanted to linger, to admire them, and he wished Emily were here by his side. It seemed wrong to be without her, both because of the nature of his visit to the mine, but more importantly because of the horses. The mustangs were special. Wild. Untamed. As much as Emily loved horses, she would have delighted in the mustangs. He smiled, imagining her sketching them.

If only it weren't raining.

And if only she were here.

"I would like to have mustangs on my ranch," Baron mused. "I'd relish the sight of them grazing in my fields."

David pressed his lips together. "If we start the mine up, it will pollute the river. I'm not sure what I'll do with the horses. I might need to..."

"Hey, what's the hold-up?" came a shout from the back of the buckboard.

David sighed, snapped the reins and they set off again, heading for the mines. "My father wouldn't have approved of the horses. He never liked to have anything around that wasn't earning its keep."

"I understand. Money makes the world go around."

"I don't know about that," David said. "Sometimes a man needs to do what's right. Not what brings in the most money."

Baron snorted. "Make enough money, son, and you can have whatever you want."

"My father made plenty of money and his wealth made him foolish. He squandered a fortune. I don't want to recoup the money so much for myself, but for others." He tilted his head in the direction of the mare and foal. "I enjoy caring for the wild horses even though they don't make me a dime."

"I know of a way you can come into a great deal of money," Charles yelled from the back of the buckboard. "You just need to marry the right girl."

David frowned but said nothing.

Baron chuckled at Charles's suggestion. Everyone riding on the buckboard knew of the man's desperation to rid himself of his daughter. Charles had tried foisting her off on at least half of the men over the course of the morning.

"Katherine stands to inherit a small fortune," Charles continued, undaunted, his speech slightly slurred.

"She's a pretty enough girl," David said.

"Now you've done it," Baron muttered. "You've encouraged him. After that comment, you won't hear the end of Katherine's virtues."

Fortunately, one of the men distracted Charles with a question regarding a legal matter and they were able to make the rest of the trip in relative peace. The rain let up as they drew close to the mine entrance. Baron thought this would be good news, but David muttered a few words under his breath about the rain-soaked hillside.

"What's the matter?" Baron asked.

"The entrance of the new shaft has collapsed. We'll have to use the old entry. I hadn't intended to use that one again."

Baron followed David's gaze and saw what he meant. A pile of rocks and debris marked the spot where the new entrance had once been. Thirty paces away stood a low entrance, partly supported by cracked and crumbling wooden beams.

"It'll be fine, boy," Charles urged. "Baron just wants a quick look to make certain the mine actually exists. We can take a quick look and turn back to meet the ladies for lunch."

David kept his full attention on Baron as if waiting for a signal to stay or go. Everyone knew it was Baron's stamp of approval that would set things in motion. If he didn't care for some aspect of the operation, the mine might never again be a working mine.

Nobody spoke while Baron surveyed the rocky hillside. He rubbed his jaw, thinking about how hard he'd worked to get to this point in his life. The men riding behind him came from wealth and privilege. He was nothing more than a man who had his start in life shoveling coal, and he relished the notion that a famed mining group needed him.

He let them wait, daring them to urge a decision from him. Finally, he spoke. "I want to see the mine, and I want to see it today. We'll use the old entrance."

Chapter Twenty-Seven

Emily

Virginia seemed restless and bored of merely sitting and chatting. Emily noticed that the woman had a nervous energy about her. She had a quick mind too, a pleasing trait considering the long hours she'd had to endure in her company. Emily couldn't say the same about the Stanton ladies. They flitted from subject to subject, never lingering long enough to plumb the depths.

Sarah said little, merely glancing out the windows every chance she got. Her expression grew more fretful. Her face lost what little color it had and yet her features still retained a fragile beauty.

Even Virginia noticed Sarah's fretfulness. Eventually she stopped baiting the girl. To pass the time, she offered to take the ladies on a tour of the Whittier home. The notion didn't interest Emily, particularly, but the Stanton women seemed pleased with the idea. Emily could almost picture the tally forming in their minds as they imagined Katherine one day taking ownership.

As she walked through the grand home, Emily's skin prickled uncomfortably. She'd only met Orson a handful of times and had tried to banish the memory of him from her mind. It felt unpleasant to be in his home and amongst his possessions even if Virginia didn't know about Emily and Orson's connection.

One of the servants came upstairs to ask Virginia about the lunch.

"It's getting late, isn't it?" Virginia muttered. "I told David we should feed our guests before they go tramping across the ranch."

"They should be back by now," Sarah said. "David... I mean, Mr. Whittier, told me they would only look inside the new entrance to show Mr. Calhoun the improvements."

"He probably couldn't resist showing off the silver deposits." Virginia turned to dismiss the servant. "Tell cook that we'll eat in a quarter hour. I would like to show the ladies Ozzie's study before we dine."

They walked down the grand staircase, through the lavish marbled entrance and into what Emily assumed was the study. The first thing she saw was a mahogany desk. Dominating the room, it spoke of a man who enjoyed fine things.

"Is it imported?" Mrs. Stanton asked as she ran her fingers along the elegantly carved edge.

"Of course. My husband always insisted on having the finest of everything. He didn't care who he hurt acquiring precisely what he desired."

A chill crawled across Emily's skin. Turning, she found Virginia staring directly at her, her eyes carefully appraising her. Silence stretched between them, while the two Stanton women chattered about the fine Persian rugs.

"How lucky for you that Mr. Whittier had such refined taste," Mrs. Stanton said. "Charles grumbles at each of my purchases no matter how modest."

"Daddy is tight-fisted," Katherine said with a sigh. "He thinks I should wear the same dress to two different balls. I don't know why he gets so angry when I ask for a new gown."

"It's true. Your father sometimes forgets who came into the marriage with more money. I wasn't raised to count my pennies, and I won't raise my only daughter to pinch hers."

"And you, Emily?" Virginia arched a brow. "How were you raised?"

Katherine sneered at the question and turned away, demonstrating her complete disdain for Emily. She crossed the room, moving to the fireplace. Her mother followed. They stood in front of the mantle and admired the collection of antique clocks.

"I was raised to be mindful of my spending," Emily said quietly. Her stomach churned. Her heart thundered. "I still am mindful even though my husband wants to buy me silks and gems."

"Gems?" Virginia scoffed. "Be careful with a man who wants to buy you gold and diamonds. The better the jewelry, the worse the sin."

"I'm sorry?" Emily whispered.

"If a man insists on buying you something pretty and costly, you should always ask why. If the gift comes after he's been away for any length of time, you should prepare yourself."

"Prepare myself? For what?"

"For a confession. For excuses. For heartache."

A servant entered the study. "Begging your pardon, Mrs. Whittier. Lunch is served."

"I can hardly wait to see the table settings," Katherine said.

"How many silver services do you have?" Mrs. Stanton asked.

171

"I forget," Virginia said. "Let's ask Esmeralda. She's in charge of polishing each piece."

The two Stanton ladies followed the maid out, with Sarah and Virginia close behind. Virginia stopped in the doorway to look back at Emily. The cold look had gone from her eyes, and she regarded Emily with a hint of bemusement.

Emily's blood chilled. She wondered if Virginia would take this moment to rail against her, for there was no mistaking her intent. All morning she could hardly think of Baron without missing him keenly, but now she prayed he would stay away even longer. If Virginia wanted to hurt her, she could do so very easily by calling her out. If she told the entire group about the arrangement between Orson and Emily's mother, Baron would suffer as much humiliation as she would. Perhaps even more.

"Are you coming, dear?" Virginia asked.

"In just a moment."

"Don't take too long. Mrs. Stanton is probably slipping my best serving pieces into a hidden pocket."

She smiled at her own joke, but there was something in her eyes that Emily hadn't seen before. A weary sadness. Her demeanor of light-hearted irreverence wore on her. It was a façade that cost her dearly.

"Ozzie loved this room. It might interest you to know that."

"It would?" Emily gripped the back of a nearby chair in an attempt to steady herself. "Why would I care about his favorite room?"

Virginia gestured to the paintings on the walls. "He had these paintings done over the years. That painting was the final piece he commissioned, but he never lived to see it. Sadly."

The painting held in a gilded frame was of a girl sitting on a park bench. Ducks surrounded her, pecking at the crumbs she threw. The girl smiled and gazed at the birds. She had violet eyes.

Emily stared at the painting, certain she was in the midst of a nightmare. Mr. Whittier had an image of her painted. The piece hung in his home, a permanent record of her shame.

"He was very fond of you," Virginia said.

Emily lifted a trembling hand to her mouth to stop her cry of despair.

"Perhaps I should just give the painting to you," Virginia said softly.

"I don't want it. Why would I want to be reminded of... that?"

"To remember your clever business arrangement."

"It wasn't mine. It was never mine. My mother sold me."

Virginia eyed her as if trying to determine the truth of her words.

"Would you like to know how old I am?" Emily asked.

"I can hardly see what difference that makes."

"I'm nineteen," Emily whispered.

Virginia, standing with her hand on her hip, paled. Her hand dropped from her narrow frame. They stood staring at each other as the rain drummed down on the windows. Finally, after an agonizing few moments passed, Virginia nodded.

"My mother sold me to the highest bidder when I was *fourteen*."

"I didn't know," Virginia said softly. "I had no idea."

"Neither did I. When Mr. Whittier came to discuss the arrangement with me, I threatened blackmail. It was my only hope of ending matters with him."

"He called you his investment," Virginia said.

Emily held back a cry of disgust, fighting to keep her last shred of dignity. "I can assure you that his investment, Virginia, never paid a profit."

Virginia drew a deep breath and let it out slowly. "All right, Emily. Come. Your secret is safe with me."

Chapter Twenty-Eight

Baron

Baron had to duck his head as he stepped inside the mineshaft. Cobwebs stuck to his face and he gave a grunt of irritation as he wiped them away with his sleeve. He'd been so anxious to see the mine, he'd forged ahead without waiting for the lanterns to be lit. He wasn't normally impulsive. He chided himself for his foolishness, especially since the mine could be writhing with snakes.

A moment later, David joined him holding two lanterns, one in each hand. Charles walked unsteadily beside him. Even in the dim lamplight, Baron could see the redness in Charles's eyes. Baron hadn't imagined that Charles would want to come along. He probably wanted to be sure that Baron approved of what he saw.

When no one else entered the mine, Baron furrowed his brow. "Where are the rest of the men?"

"They're concerned about using the old entrance," David said.

"Bunch of little girls." Charles waved his hand, the effort almost knocking him over.

"We're a fine group of explorers, aren't we?" Baron grumbled. "Here, give me a lantern. I don't want to meet up with a rattler down here."

"Bah! I'm not afraid of snakes!" Charles muttered.

"Who said anything about being afraid?" Baron took the lamp and shone it on the path before them. "I just have a healthy respect for them. That's all. How far down do we have to go to see a sign of silver?"

"The nearest deposit is about a hundred or so paces in. I'd say there's about forty feet of soil above you at that point."

The lamp offered little light in the choking darkness. At most the flame lit five paces in front of him, but he was not deterred. He felt a surge of anticipation as he set off, heading straight into the inky black. The air grew cooler as they descended. Twice, Baron had to wait for David and Charles to catch up.

Finally, they reached the spot where David claimed the miners had found a silver deposit. Baron expected to see something brilliant, like points of light reflecting from the walls. He saw no such thing, just a dark wall of dirt, with some small darker patches.

Baron moved closer to the wall to get a better look and bumped his head on the ceiling. Clods of dirt fell on his head and down his collar. Any other time he might have felt the discomfort, but not now.

"Is this silver?" Barron asked, pointing to a small, dark rock.

Charles belched and swore. "Can't be. Where's the shine?"

"Silver ore is dark," David said. "It has to be melted out of the rock. It's quite a process to get to the shiny forks and knives you have on your table."

"There's hardly any here," Charles grumbled.

"The new entrance has better samples. We'll have that opened up as soon as..."

He let his words drift off. Baron knew what he waited for. The cartel needed funds to pay for improvements and general operations. David's father had mismanaged things, bungled them badly, and now the son was left to tidy up his father's mess. The rumors suggested a woman had ruined Whittier. Baron understood that all too well. His own father had been betrayed as well.

His thoughts went to Emily and he wondered what she would think of the silver ore here deep in the belly of the mine. He would never allow her to come down this far, but he liked to think that she would marvel at the sight. Perhaps the new mine would have silver closer to the surface. He'd waited for this day for so long, but the success didn't feel as glorious without her by his side.

Baron turned to his two companions. "Well, gentlemen. Shall we join the ladies for lunch?"

David nodded. "If you're ready, we can head back."

Going back up proved to be harder than expected. Dust hung in the air, choking them. Baron wondered why he hadn't noticed it on the way down. Probably because he'd been so anxious to explore the mine's depths.

"What do you think?" Charles demanded. "Are you still as enthusiastic as you were in the beginning? I'll admit I expected a larger deposit, but it still holds promise, wouldn't you say?"

"It holds promise," Baron admitted. He schooled his tone to make certain he didn't give away too much enthusiasm. The deal hadn't been formalized and until then he wanted to hold his cards close to his chest. He caught the look of disappointment on David's face.

A man's voice came from the entrance of the mine. "Halloo, is everything all right?"

"It's fine," David shouted back. "Why do you ask?"

The effort of shouting in the dusty passageway made him cough. It took him a few moments for the fit of coughing to subside. They had to halt their progress and wait during which time the man had shouted several times.

"Come again," Baron shouted.

"The new mine has had some disturbance," the man yelled. "Rocks shifted and rolled down the hillside. Is everything all right over here?"

"Dear God," David muttered. "Yes, it's fine. We'll be there soon."

His words were swallowed by a rumble as the earth shook. Charles yelped and snatched the lamp from David. Shadows danced crazily along the walls as Charles hurried ahead.

"We can't keep stopping for you, David," he shouted over his shoulder.

David started to reply, but Baron clapped his shoulder. "Let the fool go. I'll stay with you."

A rock fell from the side of the wall and tumbled down the passageway, disappearing into the darkness. David coughed again. This time he didn't stop to catch his breath. Their progress was hampered by the dust Charles had kicked up. The fact they only had one lamp didn't help matters.

The light from Charles' lamp vanished in the gloom. Baron cursed under his breath. He'd never imagined Charles Stanton was such a selfish man and vowed to dismiss him at his first chance.

The ground shook. A low roar echoed through the stone walls of the passageway. The rock crumbled around them. A boulder broke free. The huge rock rolled towards them. They tried to move out of the way, but when David screamed, Baron knew their fortune had just taken a terrible turn. He seethed with fury, cursing himself for not pulling David out of harm's way.

Dust filled the passageway, making it impossible to see anything. Baron could tell where David was by the sound of his choking cries. Moving towards the noise, he came to a quick halt, his attention fixed on the lantern. The lantern's flame flickered, sputtered and died, leaving them in utter darkness.

Chapter Twenty-Nine

Emily

"The judge wanted me to stand trial for defrauding my creditors," Virginia said, a smile playing on her lips. "But I outwitted him."

Katherine Stanton stared wide-eyed. "You fooled a judge?"

"I did. I conducted my own research at the law library of a dear friend. I came up with arguments even my legal counsel didn't know of." Virginia took a dainty bite of her sorbet. "In addition, I vowed to pay back every penny my husband owed. In doing so, I managed to avoid a trial and keep all Whittier property in my son's and my name."

Emily marveled at Virginia's poise and her intellect. Never had she met a woman so self-possessed. Virginia Whittier was a force to behold and Emily couldn't help feeling a grudging respect. Although Emily had hardly been able to eat a bite of lunch, she'd warmed slowly to Virginia's stories of overcoming her financial woes. The woman was no fool. She was shrewd, cunning and resourceful. Those traits had helped her turn her family's fortune around after Orson died. Now, it seemed, her focus was to see her son married, and married well.

The Stanton ladies understood this too, but what they couldn't see was that Virginia seemed to have a different definition of marrying well. They'd assumed it meant marrying a girl with wealth, when, in fact, Virginia wanted to see her son marry for love. Before lunch, Virginia had toyed with them, both for her own amusement and to torment Sarah. Sometime over the course of the morning, she'd tired of her game. Perhaps she'd simply felt sorry for Sarah.

Emily certainly did. She felt a sort of kinship with the quiet girl. Virginia could ruin either of them. Easily. The notion felt like a sodden weight inside her chest, making it difficult to draw a full breath. She was trapped, imprisoned on the Whittier ranch until Baron returned. And then what? Would Virginia tell him about Emily's sordid past, or would she wait for another time?

Virginia promised Emily's secret was safe, but was she a woman of her word?

The five women sat at the Whittier dining table. The men hadn't returned yet. Virginia hadn't bothered removing their place settings, telling the staff that the men would be along by and by. The women sat at one end of the long table that was presided over by Virginia Whittier.

"I was a fool to let my husband manage our family affairs," Virginia said. "A man with vices can't be trusted. They'll always love their weaknesses more than their wife or children."

She directed the words at Sarah, who blinked in confusion at being addressed with that bit of wisdom.

"Even men without vices need to be managed," Virginia said.

"I would n-never try to manage my husband," Sarah stammered.

Virginia shrugged a shoulder. "Suit yourself, but you'll need to travel with him, at the very least."

"Whom is she marrying?" Mrs. Stanton asked.

"She'll marry my son if I have any say about the matter. Once the two of them realize what everyone else knows."

Emily laughed softly, quickly covering her mouth to hide her response. Mrs. Stanton's face turned red with anger.

"Really! Mrs. Whittier, you can't be serious. You want David to wed your *maid*."

"I'm not a maid." Sarah squared her shoulders.

Emily smiled. *Good girl.*

Mrs. Stanton waved a dismissive hand. "I don't know what you are, but you have no business throwing yourself at a man who is so far above you."

"I didn't throw myself at him," Sarah defended. "Not like your daughter."

"What?" Mrs. Stanton screeched.

"Look at her dress," Sarah demanded. "She's paraded into the house like some floozy on display."

Virginia directed a bemused glance at Emily.

"Floozy?" Katherine screamed. "How dare you?"

Just when it looked like a full-blown brawl might break out in the middle of the Whittier dining room, shouts came from the front of the house. Charles Stanton bellowed, calling for his wife and child, his voice echoing along the hallways.

Nobody moved. Servants ran past, and Emily could hear them trying to calm Mr. Stanton to no avail. A moment later, he stepped into the doorway.

"We're leaving," his voice boomed.

"I should say so," Mrs. Stanton replied with disgust.

"Where is the rest of the group?" Virginia demanded.

"There was a problem in the mine."

Emily let out a small cry of alarm. She gripped the armrests and tried to tell herself she'd imagined the words. The mine couldn't have a problem because that would mean men were in danger. Her thoughts turned slowly in her mind as she battled shock and disbelief.

"They're trying to get the men out now," Charles said. "I'm afraid I cannot stay. I've had a terrible shock and my doctor has advised-"

"Go, you fool," Virginia hissed. "Get off my ranch before I throw you off."

The Stantons rushed from the house, shouting and arguing every step of the way. The ensuing silence hung heavily in the air. Emily's heart thudded against her chest. Her eyes prickled, and she wanted to wipe the tears before they fell, but her hands wouldn't obey her.

Sarah got to her feet and regarded them both with a solemn look. "Well, ladies. We won't be much help to the men if we don't get moving."

"You're right, Sarah." Virginia's voice sounded small and distant. "We need to see what can be done."

Virginia ordered a buckboard to be harnessed and loaded with shovels and picks. A few cowboys rode out with them as they journeyed to the edge of the ranch where the mine lay. Virginia held the reins and drove the team expertly along the rutted path.

"Virginia," Emily said quietly.

The woman turned, a startled look in her eyes. "What is it?"

"I'm sorry."

Virginia pressed her lips together and nodded. The path climbed a rocky ridge and the horses strained against the weight. The tools rattled and clattered in the buckboard, making conversation difficult. When they reached the top, the racket faded away.

"You have no need to apologize," Virginia said. "You were hardly to blame. If anything, you were more a victim than I was, as young as you were."

Despite feeling heartsick about Baron, Emily felt a glimmer of gratitude.

Chapter Thirty

Baron

Baron skimmed his fingers over the rock. The large stone, the size of a small crate, pinned David's ankle to the floor of the passage. Any movement that Baron made, trying to shift the rock, was sure to cause the man more agony. The only blessing amid this disaster was that David had passed out from the pain.

The darkness would make things a thousand times more difficult. Vile curses spilled from Baron's mouth as he imagined what he'd do to Charles Stanton the next time he saw him.

He ran his fingers under the lower edges of the rock. Without even a shred of light, he could see nothing and there was no chance his eyes would adjust to the absolute darkness. His hand brushed against David's ankle. David groaned in response but didn't waken.

"Thank God, Emily's not with me," Baron muttered.

His heart ached as he wondered if he and David would be able to escape the mine. Without a light, he had no idea if the way was clear or blocked by rock fall. He moved around the fallen man until he reached the wall on the other side. Sitting, with his back against the wall, he positioned himself to put his feet on the rock. If he pushed hard enough, he could roll the rock off David's leg.

"Stay asleep a little longer, David."

He tested his theory with a little pressure and to his relief, felt the rock give slightly.

"I'm pretty sure you don't want to be awake for this part," he muttered. "It's going to hurt like a son of a gun."

He pushed hard, straining against the weight. Although the rock had shifted slightly, it refused to budge another inch. Sweat dripped down his forehead. He wiped his sleeve across his face and let out a growl of frustration.

"David, I hate to say this, but I'm rethinking my investment in the mine. I'd advise you to do the same."

He tore his coat off and flung it aside. It landed nearby, causing a few pebbles to tumble past. The error with his plan had been that he needed to position himself closer to the rock, so he could push harder. He moved a few rocks behind him, reducing the distance between him and David. His hand brushed against the side of the wall a little lower down the passage. With a start, he realized the lower spot would be a better place to sit. He could move the rock without risking it rolling over David's foot. Maybe. If he was wrong, the rock might roll over David's foot and crash against him. It was the only way. He hated risking his own safety, not out of selfish reasons but because it would make David's rescue even more unlikely. His leg needed medical attention.

Despite the risk to himself, Baron shifted his spot to the lower position.

"We should say a prayer," David said.

Baron snorted. "You're awake?"

There was no reply.

"David?"

Nothing.

Baron groaned and let his head fall back. While he was a believer, he rarely prayed. The only time he prayed was when he went to church to hear Henry give a sermon. He tried to imagine what Henry would say or do in his place but couldn't come up with any reasonable ideas. His mind was moving slowly. Maybe because of the thick, dank air.

"God, please help me move this rock."

His words were greeted with silence.

He positioned his feet against the rock and drew a shaking breath. "And don't let me make it worse." He coughed, cleared his throat and added, "please."

With that, he pushed with all his might. With the first push, his feet slipped. He tried again with no results. His heart pounded inside his chest with the effort of pushing the rock and trying to breathe. He sucked in a lungful of air and heaved with all his might. The rock rolled away and proceeded to tumble past, picking up speed as it moved down the route. A moment later the boulder crashed against a rock wall, the sound echoing along the passageway.

Baron held his breath, waiting to see if the impact would cause more of the mine to crumble. When nothing happened, he got to his feet. Reaching down, he clasped David's coat and heaved him up to a sitting position. From there, he lifted him over his shoulder. It would be slow going, and Baron would have to be careful not to scrape David's body against the roof of the passage. But at least they were free of the heavy rock.

Baron began his trek up the passage, one arm wrapped around David's lower body, the other hand on the wall, feeling in the darkness for low ceilings, and rubble. His movements were slow, but he made steady progress. He felt a small shred of satisfaction that he managed to not bang David against the rock wall or ceiling.

He tried to recall how long the passage was. David had told him, but Baron had been too eager to catch a glimpse of the silver to pay much attention. He chided himself for his rashness. He'd been blind to the danger and risk, thinking only of the riches.

Each breath burned his lungs. As he trudged along the passage, feeling each inch of the way, his thoughts slowed and became fixed on the one thing he wanted to see more than anything else. Emily. He pictured her in his mind, heard her soft, feminine laugh and recalled her sweet scent.

"I don't want a mine. I want mustangs," he said. The sound of his voice startled him. He chuckled at his foolishness and resolved to go back to imagining Emily. Now was not the time to imagine new ventures. He didn't want anything. Not really. Just Emily and, God-willing, a family one day. That was all. It was a simple yearning and yet it seemed so much more than he deserved.

Chapter Thirty-One

Emily

The men milled about the hillside, trying to clear the rubble. Without tools, they hadn't been able to make much progress. Emily scanned the group, searching for Baron. Her heart sank. He wasn't amongst the group which meant he was trapped in the mine. Desperation gripped her heart.

Virginia eyed them with a grim countenance. She pulled the buckboard to a halt and the women got down. The cowboys who had accompanied them hitched the team to a nearby post and secured their horses. Virginia directed the men to clear the bigger rocks, the ones that could be managed between a team of two or three. She ordered Sarah and Emily to load smaller rocks into bins that could be dragged away.

The work progressed slowly, but steadily. By late afternoon, the entrance was almost cleared. Emily prayed that there were no other rock falls inside the shaft. Every so often, Virginia would order the workers to stop. She'd call into the mine and everyone would listen intently.

Each time Virginia called and got no response, Emily felt her heart break a little more. She tried her best to keep her mind free of desperate thoughts, choosing instead to pray for the men's safety. Sarah worked beside her, at times weeping softly, but saying little.

At dusk, a wagon arrived bringing food and drink. They paused briefly, standing around a fire to eat. Tired and dirty, the ragged crew spoke little as they ate. The fire crackled and cast a glow across the faces of the workers. The men who'd come to see the mine, and possibly invest in the operation, stood beside cowboys who worked for the Whittier Family. Sarah, Virginia and Emily sat on overturned bins, too exhausted to speak.

They returned to work, weary and silent.

"Let's talk about something happy," Emily said.

Sarah winced as she lifted a stone and let it fall into the bin. "Mrs. Whittier wants me to marry David."

"I believe you're right." Emily smiled, grateful for a small scrap of conversation. "Do you love him?"

"I do. Very much."

"And he loves you?"

"He says he does."

They pulled the bin to the side and dumped out the rocks.

"I didn't want him to regret marrying a girl who was beneath him."

"I see. Well, that's for the best."

Sarah was about to pick up another rock but stopped and stared in shock.

Emily gave her a gently teasing smile. "Just think how happy Katherine Stanton could make him."

Sarah shook her head but offered a tired smile. "I just want to see him. To tell him how much I care for him. I never did and I regret that. He thinks he needs to make the mine a success so that he has something to offer me."

Emily's heart ached. "I'd give anything to have them out of that mine. Safe. I haven't even kissed Baron."

Sarah dropped a rock into the bin where it clattered against the others. "You haven't kissed him today?"

Emily pursed her lips, fighting a sudden flood of tears that threatened to fall. She turned away to hide her sorrow. A moment later, she managed a choked reply. "Not today. Or ever."

Chapter Thirty-Two

Baron

Baron's body ached. His lungs burned. The effort of carrying a man up a sloping passageway made each breath painful. He considered stopping to rest but discarded the notion.

David needed help. While Baron would have relished a small reprieve, each moment he rested would prolong David's misery. Baron wanted to get David out and he wanted to see Emily. With those two simple goals, he trudged onward.

David stirred and groaned. "I'm sorry, Mr. Calhoun."

"S'fine," Baron grunted.

"My father wasn't a good man."

Baron wondered if David was delusional from pain. Why would he talk about his father at a time like this? Baron hardly cared if the man had been a good man or a scoundrel. He'd heard about him but didn't give much credence to rumor.

"He was ruled by lust."

"Sorry...to...hear."

While it wasn't easy to hold a conversation, talking with David made the blind journey along the passage a little easier. The silence had been unnerving. He moved with greater determination, making quicker progress.

"My mother never forgave him."

"Right."

"He said he never touched her."

Baron banged his leg against a boulder. He snarled from the jolt of pain and groaned with the effort of stepping over the rock. If he had been alone, the task would have been difficult, climbing in complete darkness up the mineshaft. But carrying a full-grown man, who needed to be spared further impacts, was nearly impossible.

"Don't blame her," David said.

The man had to be hallucinating, Baron decided. He was out of his mind with pain. This wasn't the first time he'd seen a man lose his wits because of an injury. He'd seen more than his share of violence when he worked amongst the outlaws of West Texas.

Maybe it was his imagination, but the air felt cooler against his skin. His clothes, damp from perspiration, clung to his frame. He noticed a slight draft and tried not to get his hopes up. He had no idea how long he'd been toiling, each step forward in the darkness seeming to take several minutes. Maybe he neared the mine's opening.

"Violet was so young. Too young."

Baron grimaced. Suddenly the exchange felt as though it might lead to some sordid confession. He didn't want to know Whittier's secrets. Besides, what did it matter? David likely wanted to lighten his conscience. Baron felt a pang of sympathy. While he hadn't been proud of the way his father gave up on his life, his father never shamed him.

"Her mother sold her."

Baron's skin prickled with a sense of something terrible to come. "Violet?"

"That's what he called her. Violet. Because of her eyes."

Baron could hardly make sense of the words. It couldn't be possible. Emily and David's father? He gritted his teeth. His hold on David slipped and he almost dropped his passenger. By sheer grit, he managed to keep moving.

Because of her eyes...

Emily, his Emily. He pictured her fearful response when she'd met David. He recalled the way she'd begged him not to leave her at the house. He growled softly, imagining her in the home of Virginia Whittier, waiting for him to return. He doubled his efforts to move quickly along the length of the dark mineshaft, needing to get his sights on Emily more urgently than anything he'd ever needed before.

"Does your mother know?" he asked.

"She knows."

Baron snarled with fury. He'd left Emily in a terrible position and prayed Virginia Whittier hadn't harmed her. Surely the woman was furious. Would she take revenge on Emily even though she didn't have anything to do with the arrangement?

"She blames my father."

Baron said nothing, praying that David was telling him the truth.

Chapter Thirty-Three

Emily

The last rays of dusk faded. The sky darkened from a deep violet to a velvety black. Stars appeared, blanketing the sky. The men lit torches and set them out amidst the workers. When there was enough of a gap in the entrance, Virginia took a torch in hand and stepped inside. One of the cowboys tried to talk her out of entering the mine, but she brushed off his concerns.

"This mine still belongs to me. I'll be the one to assume the risk."

She vanished inside the entrance. Emily watched the shadows dance and the light fade as Virginia made her way into the mine. Sarah covered her eyes and grimaced. Emily took her other hand and gripped it tightly as she said a prayer that the men and Virginia would emerge safely, and soon.

They waited for what felt like an eternity. A shadow and then a flicker of light announced Virginia's return. She stepped out of the cave, her face wreathed in a bright smile. A figure emerged behind her. A man carrying the body of another man.

Suddenly, the hillside was a hive of activity as the men rushed forward to help. They eased the man to the ground. It was David, hurt but alive. Virginia knelt beside him and spoke words of comfort while two of the men studied his injured leg.

Sarah pushed through the crowd and went to his side. She crouched beside him, taking his hand in hers.

"His leg is broken," one of the men announced.

"Bring the wagon," Virginia shouted.

The men loaded him onto the buckboard and helped Sarah up. She sat down beside him. David laid his head on her lap as the buckboard departed.

With David on his way home, Emily searched out her husband. In the flickering torchlight, he threaded his way through the group. She made her way past the group of onlookers, feeling as though she moved through a dream.

He gave her a weary smile. "Either you're my wife, or you're one of heaven's angels."

His voice, a harsh rasp, sounded both terrible and wonderful. Her heart thrilled to hear him speak. Her breath caught with the disbelief that he stood before her, safe and sound. She shook her head, cupping his jaw with her hand. "I'm your wife. Just your wife."

The firelight cast a glow across his dusty features. Grit scratched the palm of her hand. He covered her hand with his.

"Are you all right, my love?" he asked.

She shook her head and laughed softly. "Am *I* all right? Of course, I am."

He closed his eyes as if reveling in her words. She couldn't understand why he would ask if she were all right. After all, he was the one who had just emerged from a partially collapsed mine.

"I'm fine," she said gently. "Just so very relieved to see my husband."

"Are you mine, Emily?"

"Baron," she whispered. "I'm yours if you want me."

"Is that so?" he asked softly.

"It is." She swallowed, trying to dislodge the lump in her throat. "I have something I need to tell you. About my past."

"I don't care, Emily. You just agreed you're mine. There's nothing you can say that will change that." He wiped his face with his sleeve, grimacing as he tried to clean off some of the grime. "I'm sure I look like hell."

"I think you look heroic."

He pulled her into his arms, wrapping her in his embrace. Lifting her chin, he lowered, pausing just a fraction of an inch from her lips. She let herself sink into his arms, relishing the feel of his powerful presence. "I think you should kiss me, then."

She gave a breathless laugh. "You do?"

"I've had a hard day, Emily."

"My word," she whispered. "You have had a hard day."

"All I could think about was escaping that cave, so I could kiss my wife. It's what kept me going."

She clasped the back of his neck as he leaned down for a kiss. Both of them were covered in dust and dirt, but she didn't care. His lips brushed hers. He held her even closer and pressed his mouth to hers, holding her there for a suspended, astonishing moment.

The kiss was perfect.

He held her firmly as if he feared that she might try to escape his hold. Instead, she melted into his arms, eager to submit to his tender touch.

When they broke the kiss, he smiled, gazing into her eyes for a long moment. Despite the dirt that clung to him, she'd never thought him more handsome. His eyes held a warmth she'd never seen. His touch held a tenderness she'd never felt. His voice held a gentle tone she'd never heard.

The starlit sky framed his face and broad shoulders, and Emily was certain she'd never known such happiness.

Chapter Thirty-Four

One month later...

Baron

Emerging from the ocean, Baron scanned the beach for Emily. A moment before she'd sat on a blanket under an umbrella, sketching contentedly. Now she was gone. He heard her laughter and spied her chasing after a piece of paper as it blew across the sand. She snatched it, but then a gust of wind blew her hat away. Her shriek brought a smile to his face as he jogged to the sandy stretch in front of the hotel.

Her bonnet tumbled along the sand. He reached the hat before she did. He offered it to her, but before she could take the hat, he pulled it out of her reach. Instead of giving it to her, he held it behind his back, taunting her.

"You'll have to come take it from me."

"Baron, you scoundrel. Give me my hat."

He frowned. "For a price."

She gave him a playful smile. "Your prices seem to be getting higher, Mr. Calhoun. This morning you made me kiss you while you shaved."

He shrugged and twirled the hat on his finger. "That was hours ago. I'd like another kiss for my trouble."

She folded her arms across her chest, giving him a sweet pout, but shaking her head, refusing him. The wind blew her hair free, tugging at her pins and leaving a lovely disarray in its wake. He could look at her all day, feasting his eyes on her lovely face, beautiful eyes and...

His gaze dipped to her mouth. She still wore an impudent pout which made him want to kiss her even more. He'd kiss the sass from her right here on the beach. Earlier that morning there had been numerous families enjoying the water. Most had returned to the hotel for lunch and probably a nap.

"My skin starts to get pink in no time, Baron. You're being ungentlemanly."

She chided him, but the glint of humor in her eyes gave her away.

"Maybe I am, but you could have anything you want from me with just a kiss." He dangled the bonnet, teasing her. "It's right here, for a kiss, it's yours."

"You're dripping wet. I'll kiss you later."

"I don't offer credit."

A gust of wind whooshed, tugging the last bit of order from her hair. She yelped and tried to brush her hair out of her face, but it was useless. The breeze made her tresses dance and swirl. Baron chuckled at her cry of indignation.

"Your fault, Mr. Calhoun," she sputtered. "I blame you entirely. And I'll blame you later when I try to comb the tangles free. How can I walk through the hotel, looking like a..."

Her words trailed off as she struggled to find the right description.

"You look beautiful." He stepped closer, brushed the wild locks from her face and smiled down at her. "You always look beautiful."

She gave him a gentle smile. "Thank you, Baron. That's very sweet of you." She stroked his jaw, but she touched him just to distract him, for in the next instant, she plucked her bonnet from his hand. Whirling away, she darted across the sand, laughing at her clever trick.

He charged after her, catching her easily, scooping her into his arms. Shrieking, wide-eyed, she banged on his shoulder with her fist. Her outrage only made him laugh.

"Put me down. Baron! Your swim clothes are soaking wet. You'll get me wet! I'm dressed for lunch."

"You should have thought of that before you played a trick on me."

Carrying her in his arms, he marched towards the shore. Slowly it dawned on Emily. Understanding drifted over her features as she realized what he intended. The threat he'd made about tossing her in the waves had been a subject of several jokes as they traveled west.

"You wouldn't dare." She clung to his neck, tightening her grip with each step.

"No?"

She struggled to free herself, writhing in his arms. Her efforts made him laugh, and his laughter sparked more of her fury. When she tried to twist free, he growled at her and she went still in his arms. She blinked in astonishment.

"Did you just growl at your wife?"

"I did." He splashed through the surf.

Now that they'd reached the water, her concern grew. She gave him a pleading look. He ignored her and continued into the ocean, stopping when the water reached almost to his waist.

"I demand a kiss," he said.

"This is utterly monstrous."

He shrugged and took a half-step further into the water.

"Baron Calhoun!" she blurted, trying to sound angry, but failing. Instead, she sounded alarmed.

"Kiss me."

She shook her head. "I refuse to give in to blackmail."

A wave splashed against him. She jerked in his arms and giggled despite her attempts to glower at him. The sound of her laugh made him happier than anything else in the world. He lived to make her smile and laugh, wanting only to give her a lifetime of happiness. Her smile faded as she gazed into his eyes. She cupped his jaw and stroked him with a gentle touch.

"I love you, Baron."

He nodded. "I know, and I'm glad. I love you too."

She leaned closer and pressed her lips to his. The kiss was a warm, lingering kiss that made his heart beat quicken. Her kisses unraveled a hard knot inside him, a tangle he'd never realized existed.

"Your kisses are salty, Mr. Calhoun."

He rested his forehead against hers and closed his eyes. "And your kisses are perfect, Mrs. Calhoun."

Epilogue

One year later...

Emily

Soft candlelight flickered, casting shadows across the nursery walls. Emily listened to the soft breath of her infant daughter, sleeping in her arms. The baby's curls framed her sweet face.

Now and again, the wind gusted around the ranch house, heralding the Blue Norther Baron had predicted. It blew past the window. She was grateful for the warm water bottle she'd set in the baby's cradle. Tonight, when the temperatures dropped, the baby would be warm, nestled in her bed.

Emily would seek out the warmth of her husband's arms during the chilly night. Sleeping next to Baron comforted her and kept her warm during the long winter nights. She'd never imagined how much she would desire his embrace, not only during the day, but while she slumbered as well.

From across the hall, the sound of another baby's soft laugh brought a smile to Emily's lips. The sound of children filled her heart with joy, especially at this time of year, the night before Christmas. It was her second Christmas as Mrs. Baron Calhoun, but her first as a mother, and first as an aunt.

To everyone's surprise, Elizabeth and Henry had also been blessed with a baby. Henry Junior had come into the world, defying the doctors who had promised Elizabeth she couldn't conceive.

Emily laid Adeline in her crib. She reached for a blanket, but the sound of the door distracted her. Baron entered the nursery with his finger raised to his lips. Coming to her side, he took over the task of putting the baby to bed. He wrapped the blanket around the sleeping child, tucking the end under the warm water bottle. For a long moment, they stood side-by-side and watched the child sleep.

Sweet Adeline...

Baron's grandmother had been called Adeline. Emily had suggested the name for their baby in the days before her birth. Somehow, she'd known the baby would be a girl. She knew that Baron wanted to make peace with his past and to honor his father in some small way. And so it was that their baby girl, born with her mother's eyes and her father's steely nature, was named Adeline.

"She's beautiful," he whispered, as he did each night when he came to tuck the blanket around his child.

"She is," Emily agreed as she always did.

Baron took Emily's hand and led her from the nursery. As they walked down the hallway, Emily caught the scent of pine from their Christmas tree downstairs. The fragrance brought a rush of pleasure to her thoughts.

In the morning, they'd have breakfast in the dining room, with a blaze crackling in the fireplace. After, they'd gather around the tree and open presents. Last year, Baron's lavish gifts embarrassed her, and this year, she was sure he'd outdo himself, showering her, Adeline and Elizabeth's family with presents.

"Everyone needs to go to bed," he grumbled good-naturedly. "Or else St. Nick won't be able to bring his gifts."

"Is that so? I'm not sure little Henry understands this principle. I heard him laughing with his parents in the guest suite."

"I already spoke with them. They promised to be abed by ten." He glanced at the clock on the mantle. "That gives them another hour. Otherwise…"

He didn't finish. A mischievous grin belied his ominous words.

Emily stepped into her dressing room, changed into her gown and hurried to bed, shivering in the cold night air. "Otherwise what?"

Baron stirred the glowing embers in the fireplace. When he tossed several pieces of wood onto the grate, sparks shot up, sizzling and crackling as they flew.

"Otherwise, everyone gets nothing more than a lump of coal." He came to bed, settling beneath the blankets and pulling her into his embrace. "Even you, Mrs. Calhoun."

"My word," she said. "I'd better go to sleep then."

He rose up on one elbow. Looking down at her he cupped her jaw and stroked her face. In the light of the fire, she watched as his gaze softened. Neither spoke as they shared a tender moment. He lowered, brushed his lips across hers, and whispered, "Give me a kiss, Emily."

And she did.

The End

Book Three of Mail Order Bluebonnet Brides
Mail Order Faith

Magnolia, Texas, 1880 – A Mail Order Bride's Secret Journey.

Faith O'Brian journeys to Magnolia without telling a soul.
Before she agrees to marry, she wants to be certain her
husband to-be is an honorable man.

Thomas Bentley tells her he's a rancher. He tells her he's a
widower with a son, a boy who desperately wants a mother. But
Thomas never mentions that he's also the sheriff of Magnolia.
The news comes as a bit of a surprise.

Books by Charlotte Dearing

The Bluebonnet Brides Collection
Mail Order Grace
Mail Order Rescue
Mail Order Faith
Mail Order Hope
Mail Order Destiny

Brides of Bethany Springs Series
To Charm a Scarred Cowboy
Kiss of the Texas Maverick
Vow of the Texas Cowboy
The Accidental Mail Order Bride
Starry-Eyed Mail Order Bride
An Inconvenient Mail Order Bride
Amelia's Storm

Mail Order Providence
Mail Order Sarah
Mail Order Ruth

and many others...

Sign up at www.charlottedearing.com to be notified of
special offers and announcements.

Printed in Great Britain
by Amazon

39643483R00128